CAPITAL MYSTERIES

Capital Mysteries
Collection

Capital Mysteries Collection

by Ron Roy

A STEPPING STONE BOOK™

Random House 🏠 New York

Who Cloned the President?
Text copyright © 2001 by Ron Roy
Illustrations copyright © 2001 by Random House, Inc.

Kidnapped at the Capital
Text copyright © 2002 by Ron Roy
Illustrations copyright © 2002 by Random House, Inc.

The Skeleton in the Smithsonian
Text copyright © 2003 by Ron Roy
Illustrations copyright © 2003 by Timothy Bush

A Spy in the White House
Text copyright © 2004 by Ron Roy
Illustrations copyright © 2004 by Timothy Bush

Map copyright © 2003 by Timothy Bush

All rights reserved.
Published in the United States by Random House Children's Books, a division of Random House, Inc., New York.
Random House and the colophon are registered trademarks and A Stepping Stone Book and the colophon are trademarks of Random House, Inc.

Visit us on the Web!
www.steppingstonesbooks.com
www.randomhouse.com/kids

Educators and librarians, for a variety of teaching tools, visit us at
www.randomhouse.com/teachers

Library of Congress Cataloging-in-Publication Data for these titles is available on request.
Who Cloned the President?
ISBN 978-0-307-26510-4 (trade) — 978-0-307-46510-8 (lib. bdg.)
Kidnapped at the Capital
ISBN 978-0-307-26514-2 (trade) — 978-0-307-46514-6 (lib. bdg.)
The Skeleton in the Smithsonian
ISBN 978-0-307-26517-3 (trade) — 978-0-307-46517-7 (lib. bdg.)
A Spy in the White House
ISBN 978-0-375-82557-6 (trade) — 978-0-375-92557-3 (lib. bdg.)

ISBN 978-0-375-85801-7

Printed in the United States of America   10 9 8 7 6 5 4 3 2 1

Contents

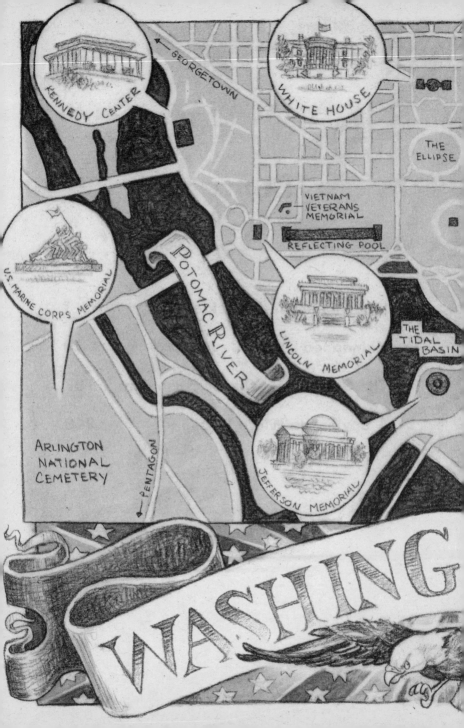

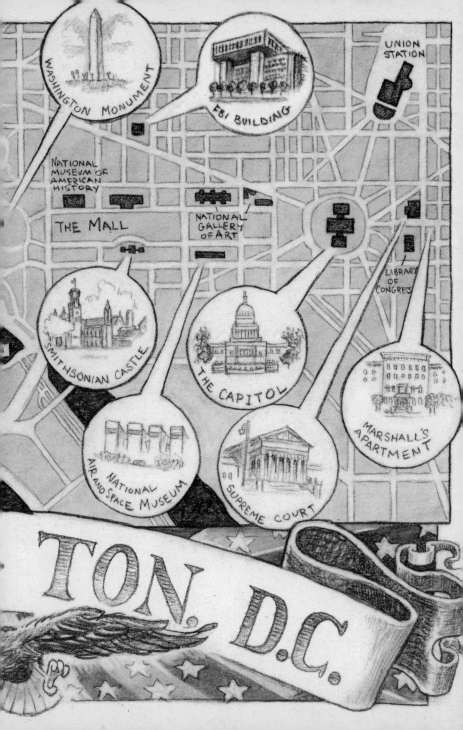

WHO CLONED THE PRESIDENT?

by Ron Roy

illustrated by Liza Woodruff

1

KC's Discovery

KC Corcoran pulled a slip of paper out of her teacher's baseball cap. She read the words on the paper and grinned.

"Who did you get, KC?" Mr. Alubicki asked.

"President Thornton," KC said.

"No fair!" Marshall Li protested. "You already know everything about him."

Mr. Alubicki smiled and passed the hat to Marshall, KC's best friend. Marshall picked a slip. "Herbert Hoover?" he said. "I don't even know who he is!"

"But you'll know all about him after you write your report," his teacher said.

Mr. Alubicki finished passing the hat around the room. "Okay, everyone, have a great weekend. Get started on your president reports. We'll discuss them Monday."

KC grabbed her backpack and followed Marshall out the door. They walked home together every day.

KC and Marshall lived in the same ten-story building in Washington, D.C. It stood between a pet shop and a Chinese restaurant.

They stopped on the way home to watch puppies and kittens through the pet-shop window.

"Why is everyone so crazy about furry animals?" Marshall asked. "Spiders make great pets, too!"

KC laughed. "Marsh, you can't cuddle up with a spider."

"Who says you can't?" Marshall asked. "I wish Mr. A. would let us write about insects instead of presidents."

Marshall loved anything with more than four legs. He kept jars of crawly things in his bedroom. Spike, his pet tarantula, slept in one of Marsh's old baseball caps.

"Presidents' Day is in February," KC reminded her friend. "If we had an insects' day, Mr. A. would let you write about Spike."

"Spike's not an insect," Marshall said. "Tarantulas are spiders, and spiders are arachnids."

"I know, I know," KC said as she pushed open the glass door of their building. "You've told me a hundred times!"

"And you still don't remember," grumbled Marshall. He pushed the elevator button.

Donald, the building manager, opened the elevator door. Donald ran the elevator and helped people get taxis out front.

"Hi, kids," Donald said. "Got plans for the weekend?"

"We have to write reports," Marshall told him. "About dead presidents."

"Mine's not dead," KC told Donald. "I picked President Thornton!"

Donald smiled as he pressed the button for Marshall's floor. "Lucky you! Maybe you'll see him around town."

Marshall got off on the third floor, and Donald took KC to the fifth. She let herself into the apartment with her key.

Lost and Found, her two kittens, came skidding across the wood floor when the door opened. KC rubbed their bellies, then headed for the kitchen.

A note was taped to the fridge.

KC—I'll be home around six. Have a snack. Love, Mom.

KC grabbed a banana and walked into the living room. Lost and Found scurried after her. She pulled *Your Presidents* from a bookshelf and looked up President Thornton.

"Listen," she said to the kittens. "Zachary Thornton had five brothers and sisters. He raised chickens and sold eggs to help his family." Then the caption of a picture caught her eye. "As a Boy Scout, Zachary Thornton earned twelve merit badges," she read.

"See, Marshall was wrong," KC mumbled. "I don't know everything about

President Thornton. I had no idea he got twelve badges in Scouts."

KC marked the page, then switched on her mom's computer. She logged on to the Internet and found more about President Thornton. "Zachary Thornton is our fourth left-handed president," KC read.

"Cool. We're both left-handed!" KC said. She kept reading and noticed a headline from *The Washington Post* newspaper. "President Thornton Says No to Human Cloning."

KC read the rest of the paragraph about scientists cloning animals. Marshall had told her that some scientists wanted to clone humans.

"I'm glad the president said no," she said. "I only want one of me!"

KC shut off the computer and turned

on the TV. She flopped on the sofa and pulled the kittens onto her lap.

Cindy Sparks, the White House reporter, was just signing off.

"Someday that'll be me," KC told her kittens. She planned to become a TV anchorwoman after college.

KC peeled the banana and channel surfed. She found a live special on President Thornton at a press conference in the White House.

"Tomorrow morning," said President Thornton, "I will make an announcement that will change human life forever."

Then someone handed the president a stack of papers. He signed them slowly, as if he were tired. He didn't smile or talk to anyone around him. He just took a paper, signed it, and reached for another.

Hmmm, thought KC. *It's not like him to be so quiet and serious. He looks sick.*

KC noticed something else. "That's weird," she said. She called Marshall and told him to turn on channel 3.

"It's the president," Marshall said a few seconds later. "So?"

"Do you see anything weird?"

"Like what?"

"Marsh, he's signing those papers with his right hand!"

Marshall laughed. "You called to tell me the president is right-handed?"

"No, he's *left*-handed!"

"Oooh, let's call 911," Marshall said.

KC kept staring at the president on TV. Signing with the wrong hand. Looking tired and way too serious. Almost like a different person. . . .

Her imagination kicked in. What if this guy was a fake? What if the real president had been kidnapped? What if he'd been drugged or . . . KC shook her head.

She could almost hear her mom warning her—for the millionth time—not to jump to conclusions.

Then she remembered that headline: "President Thornton Says No to Human Cloning."

"That's it!" KC cried.

"Marshall, get up here right now!" she yelled into the phone. "Someone cloned the president!"

2
The Plan

A few minutes later, KC's doorbell rang. She let Marshall in.

"All right," he said. He threw himself onto the sofa. "Tell me why you think the president has been cloned."

KC sat in the chair by Marshall. "You don't believe me? Look!" On the TV, President Thornton continued to sign papers. "He's signing papers with his right hand!"

Marshall stared at KC. "That means he was cloned? Maybe he hurt his left hand."

"There's other stuff, Marsh," KC said. She pointed to the TV just as the president stood up. He walked away without saying a word. "Don't you think that's weird?" asked KC. "He didn't smile or shake hands or anything. He acts like I did when I had the flu!"

"So, maybe he has the flu."

KC glared at Marshall. "Having the flu wouldn't make him sign papers with his other hand!" she said. "Something is wrong with him!"

Marshall glanced at the TV screen. The president was gone. Reporters were packing up to leave. "He did look a little different," Marshall admitted.

"He looked different because it wasn't him!" KC said. "It was a clone!"

Marshall stared at KC for a minute. "Okay," he finally said. "Let's say you're right. The President of the United States has been cloned. Who did it? Why? When?"

KC paced back and forth in front of the sofa. "I don't know! Don't try to confuse me," she said. "But that guy on TV didn't act the way our president acts. I know, Marshall. I watch him every night!" KC kept pacing.

"You're making me dizzy," Marshall said.

"Shhh, I'm thinking," KC said. She stopped pacing. "Got it!"

Marshall slumped into the sofa pillows. "I don't think I want to hear this," he muttered.

"Listen, I'll tell my mom I'm sleeping at your apartment tonight. You tell your parents you're sleeping here."

"Why?"

KC shoved him toward the door. "I'll tell you later. Meet me downstairs in five minutes!"

"But wh—?"

"And bring a jar of your spiders!"

Before Marshall could say another word, KC slammed the door. Grinning, she ran to the kitchen. She wrote a note for her mom, then grabbed some snacks from the fridge.

She charged into her bedroom and dumped the school stuff out of her backpack. She tossed in the snacks, a flashlight, her Swiss Army knife, and a tape recorder. At the last minute, she opened her bank and took out a fistful of money.

She grabbed a jacket, said good-bye to her kittens, then let herself out of the apartment.

Donald opened the elevator door. "Going out again, KC?"

"Me and Marshall are doing some research for our reports," she said.

It's not a total lie, thought KC. She paced as she waited for Marshall in the lobby.

When he showed up with his backpack, KC dragged him outside.

"Did you bring the spiders?" she asked, heading toward the bus stop.

"Yeah, but where are we going?"

"To help the president. He needs us."

Marshall stopped walking. "KC, I've known you practically my whole life. But you're acting weird. Why does the president need two fourth graders?"

The number 6 bus stopped. KC dropped quarters into the box, then pulled Marshall into a seat.

"I'm waiting," Marshall said.

KC glanced around her. The bus was nearly empty.

"Okay, I think the guy on TV was a fake or a clone," KC whispered. "If he is, what happened to the real president?"

Before Marshall could open his mouth, KC went on. "Marshall, the president is in danger! And we're going to save him!"

Marshall shook his head. "I'm in my bed. I'm having a terrible nightmare."

KC opened her eyes innocently. "All I want to do is help my country!"

Marshall stared glumly out the window. "Another question," he said. "We both lied about where we're sleeping tonight. So, where are we really sleeping?"

KC grinned. "In the White House."

3
Spider Surprise

The bus dropped them a short walk away from the White House.

KC looked at her watch. "That must be the last tour of the day. Let's get in line."

Since it was February, there weren't many tourists. KC grabbed Marshall's arm and joined the group.

"KC, can I ask a dumb question?" he whispered. "Why am I sneaking a jar of spiders into the White House?"

KC whispered her plan.

"Now I know you're nuts!" he hissed. "We're not going to sleep in the White House. We're going to sleep in jail!"

KC shushed him. "Just remember to throw the spiders when I give you the signal," she whispered.

"But how will I get them back?" Marshall asked. "I raised these spiders from babies! They love me!"

"Marshall, just think. Your spiders are going to save the President of the United States," KC said. "They'll be famous! Charlotte only saved a pig!"

"Charlotte who?"

KC raised her eyebrows.

"Oh," Marshall said, looking embarrassed. "*That* Charlotte. Anyway, what's your signal?"

KC thought for a moment. "Neck. When I say neck, you toss the spiders."

"Neck? How're you gonna work 'neck' into a conversation?"

"Trust me. Just be ready, okay?"

The line moved. Pretty soon KC and Marshall were inside the White House.

A woman in a blue suit met the group. "Good afternoon, everyone. My name is Debbie. I'll be your guide today. And since Lincoln's birthday was last week, we have opened the Lincoln bedroom for all tours!"

"Will we see President Thornton?" someone asked.

Debbie smiled. "I know he's in the building. Keep your eyes peeled."

Marshall smiled for the first time in an hour. "Maybe I can get the president's autograph!" he said.

In the Lincoln bedroom, the guide pointed out the paintings and antique furniture. "In Lincoln's term, this was not a bedroom. So he never slept in this magnificent bed," Debbie told the crowd.

The tourists said "oooh" a lot and asked questions.

"Open the jar," KC whispered.

Marshall stared at her. "Here? Now?"

She nodded. "Move away from me. Mix in with the crowd." She pointed to her neck. "And get ready for you-know-what!"

With a sick look on his face, Marshall went to stand behind three nuns. KC watched him stick both hands inside his backpack.

"If there are no more questions," the guide said, "we can move on to—"

"I have a question," KC said. She waved her arm like she did in school.

"Yes?" Debbie asked.

Everyone turned to look at KC. Suddenly she screamed, "SOMETHING IS ON MY *NECK!*"

She began jumping and slapping at her neck. "MY NECK! SOMETHING IS CRAWLING ON MY NECK!"

Out of the corner of her eye, she saw Marshall toss the spiders. No one else noticed. They were all staring at KC.

Then a woman screamed. "SPIDERS! THERE ARE SPIDERS IN MY HAIR!"

"Ugh!" the guide yelled. She swiped at a black spider crawling on her arm.

Suddenly there seemed to be spiders everywhere. Two dozen tourists panicked at once.

Everyone ran out of the room, screaming and slapping at their bodies.

With an unhappy look on his face,

Marshall slipped the empty jar into his backpack.

KC looked around. They were alone. She grabbed Marshall and dragged him down under the Lincoln bed.

"It worked!" KC whispered.

"And we're fourth-grade felons!" hissed Marshall. "Plus, I lost all my spiders!"

"Your spiders will be heroes," KC said.

"But we'll be prisoners," Marshall sputtered. "Why do I listen to you?"

"Because I'm your best friend," KC said, calmly opening her backpack.

"Juice?" she asked.

4
Under the Bed

KC drank her apple juice and ate raisin cookies. Marshall curled into a ball and glared at her.

"Aren't you hungry?" KC asked.

No answer.

"Are you really mad at me?"

Marshall closed his eyes.

"Okay, but there are only two more cookies!"

Marshall reached out a hand. "*If* we ever get out of here," he said, "I *might* forgive you."

They finished the rest of the snacks in silence.

KC kept checking her watch. Marshall sighed a lot and looked for his spiders. He didn't see any.

KC curled up and took a nap.

Marshall scratched at a mosquito bite on his ankle.

Hours later, a clock bonged ten times.

"Finally!" KC said. "Okay, Marsh, it's ten o'clock. Let's go." She crawled out from under the bed.

Marshall was right behind her. "Go where?" he asked, stretching his back.

The Lincoln bedroom was dark. Only a small light was on, near one of the doors.

"To rescue the president," KC said. She smiled at her best friend. "Maybe you will get that autograph," she added.

Marshall snorted. "I bet he's brushing his teeth and getting ready for bed." He slung his backpack over his shoulder. "Like we're supposed to be doing!"

KC smiled. "And the real president brushes his teeth with his left hand!"

She opened the door and peeked into the hall. Like the bedroom, it was nearly dark. Small lights shone on the portraits hanging on the walls. Vases of flowers stood on polished tables.

"Come on," KC whispered over her shoulder. She yanked on the first door knob they came to. It was locked. "Try every door," she ordered.

Just then a man in a uniform came around a corner. Luckily, he was looking at the floor, not straight ahead.

"Guard!" KC hissed. She grabbed Marshall and hurried him through a small door. It led to a set of stairs.

"Let's go down here," KC whispered.

"I need to find a bathroom," Marshall said.

KC whipped around. "Why didn't you go at home?"

"I did, but that was a long time ago. We were under that dumb bed for about a year! And besides," he added, "breaking into the White House always makes me a little nervous!"

KC started down the stairs. "Maybe there's a bathroom down here."

A few minutes later, they found themselves in a huge, dark kitchen. KC twisted a dimmer switch on the wall.

"Cool!" she said. "This must be where they cook those big state dinners!"

Marshall spied a small door. "I'm gonna see if that's a bathroom," he said.

KC looked around while she waited. The kitchen was in a basement. The floors were tiled. Instead of fancy wallpaper, the walls were painted white.

Marshall came back while KC was twirling a combination lock on an enormous freezer.

"Why do they lock everything in this place?" she muttered.

"To keep people like you out," Marshall grumbled.

They found a corridor and tried more doors.

"I'm getting tired of this," Marshall said. "Can we—"

"Shhh! I hear something!" KC whispered.

They froze and listened. Then Marshall heard it, too.

Somewhere, someone was laughing!

They tiptoed down the passageway, following the noise. Over their heads, pipes ran along the ceiling. Small lights shone down, casting shadows on the concrete floor.

"Look!" KC pointed to a partly opened door.

She heard someone laugh again. Squeezing Marshall's arm, she crept closer and peered around the door.

Then she nearly fainted.

President Zachary Thornton was slumped in a chair, just a few feet away!

5
Two Presidents

KC tugged Marshall into a dark corner. "It's him! He's in there!" she hissed.

"Who?" Marshall hissed right back.

"The president!" she whispered. "With a bunch of other guys!"

KC peeked into the room again. This time she noticed the president's eyes. They looked weird, like they did when she saw him on TV. She backed away from the door and grabbed Marshall's arm.

"Marsh, that's not the president in there. It's the clone!"

Marshall peeked into the room. "I hate to admit it, but I think you're right,"

Marshall said. "He looks like a zombie!"

"What are they doing?" KC asked.

"The clone is in pajamas and a robe," Marshall reported. "Three other guys are with him. They're smoking cigars and watching 'I Love Lucy.'"

Marshall backed away from the door. "Okay, we found the clone. Now what?"

KC opened her backpack and pulled out her tape recorder. She tiptoed back to the door. She clicked on the tape recorder. A deep voice was talking.

"We pulled it off, fellas. Everyone thinks our guy is really the president!"

Other voices joined in.

"—make millions of dollars!"

"—can't wait to see the headlines when we spring our little plan!"

KC hoped the recorder was picking up

every word. The hum of the tape told her she was getting something, at least.

She stared at the president's clone. He was slumped in a chair, wearing slippers, red pajamas, and a blue bathrobe. His eyes looked cold and dead.

Two men in dark suits sat at the table. On it were paper and pens, a small TV, and a few cans of soda. The third man stood by the clone. He was dressed in a white coat, the kind doctors wear.

Suddenly a rough hand grabbed KC by the arm. She turned around. A guard was glaring down at her. The guard's other hand was clamped on Marshall's shoulder.

"March, you two," the guard said. He shoved KC and Marshall into the room.

The three men looked up. The clone didn't budge.

"Well, what have we here?" the man in the doctor suit said. Moving like an eel, he crossed the room.

"I found 'em in the hall," the guard said, "playin' peek-a-boo outside the door!" The guard's breath smelled like sweaty sneakers. His fingers felt like iron on the back of KC's neck.

"Explain yourselves, please," the man in white said. His voice bubbled like he was under water.

"We were on a tour and got lost," KC said.

The man laughed. "A tour at ten-thirty? In the White House basement? I don't think so."

KC had never seen a scarier face. His head was totally bald. Pale blue eyes bugged out, and his teeth were yellow.

His arm shot out. "I'll just have that recorder, please."

"No you won't!" KC said. "I need it for a school report."

The man grabbed the recorder out of her hands. He pushed the REWIND button, then pressed PLAY. Everyone in the room heard the men's voices.

The man in white glared at KC. "Quite the little liar, aren't you?" he said.

"I'm not ly—"

"It's all my fault," Marshall said. "See, we were on a tour, then I decided to go look for the president." Marshall smiled innocently at the glaring men. "I wanted the president's autograph, so I talked my friend into helping me look for him."

Marshall turned to the clone. "Hi, Mr. President. Can I have your autograph?"

The clone didn't even blink.

"The brat's lying through his teeth!" one of the other men barked.

"We'll get the truth later," the man in white said. "For now, they can join our friend. Bring them to the storage room."

"May I please have my tape recorder?" KC asked. "I really need it for school."

The man in the white coat showed his yellow teeth. Then he threw the machine to the floor. When it hit, the tape ejected.

Still grinning, the man ground the tape and recorder under his foot. Soon they were nothing but mashed bits of plastic.

All the men laughed.

"Take these brats away," the man in the lab coat snapped at the guard.

The guard dragged KC and Marshall back into the dark hallway. They both struggled, but the man was too strong.

KC yelled. No one came to help.

"Shut up or you'll be sorry!" the guard snapped.

"You're the one who'll be sorry," said Marshall. "My dad is a lawyer!"

"Big deal," the man growled. "My old man's a bank robber!"

Halfway down the hall, the guard unlocked a door. He shoved Marshall and KC into a dark room.

The door slammed behind them. KC heard the lock turn.

"Are you okay?" Marshall said.

KC couldn't see him. The room was pitch-black. "Yeah, I'm all right," she said, rubbing the back of her neck. "How about you?"

"I'm okay, but what's that smell?"

Marshall asked. "It's like my dad's after-shave lotion."

"Shh, I hear something!" KC said.

Marshall leaned against her in the dark. "Don't say that. I'm scared enough!"

They both stood and listened, holding on to each other.

"Hello," a voice said from out of the darkness.

"Aaahhh!" Marshall yelled. "Someone's in here with us!"

KC dug for her flashlight and switched it on. The beam shone on a tired-looking, familiar face.

"It's okay, Marsh," KC said. "We just found President Thornton."

6
Locked In

The president blinked at the light. He looked tired. The skin under his eyes was saggy, as if he needed sleep. He was wearing a rumpled blue suit and a red tie.

"Who . . . what do you want?" he asked.

KC told the president how she had figured out that he'd been cloned, and about her plan to rescue him.

The president stared at KC. "Cloned?" he asked, rubbing the stubble on his chin.

"Did they drug you, sir?" KC asked. "Is that why you don't remember?"

The president nodded slowly. "Yes, I must have been drugged."

"By those goons who caught us?" Marshall added.

"I—I guess," the president agreed. "I can't remember."

KC shone the flashlight around the room. There was a small bed, a chair, and a radio on a table. On one side was a tiny bathroom.

"Mr. President, your clone is making an important announcement tomorrow," she said. "He's going to tell the world that it's okay to clone humans."

The president didn't say anything. *He must be exhausted,* thought KC.

"We have to stop them!" she went on. "Otherwise—"

"Otherwise those guys will run the world!" Marshall interrupted.

"Yes, stop them," the president said.

KC flashed her light on the door. "First we have to get out of here," she said.

Marshall tried the handle. "Good luck. The door's locked from the outside."

KC examined the door hinges. "Hand me my knife," she said to Marshall. He dug it out of her backpack.

KC opened the screwdriver part of her knife. She began removing the hinge screws. She stood on a chair to reach the top ones.

There were two hinges with four screws in each. It took KC five minutes, but finally she handed Marshall the last screw. "Done," she said.

KC and Marshall removed the door and leaned it against the wall.

KC peeked around the corner. The corridor was dark and empty. "Let's go."

"Shouldn't we put this door back?" Marshall asked. "What if some guard sees it off the hinges like this?"

KC and Marshall managed to set the door in its opening and replace the hinge screws. They left the door closed.

With the president walking between them, KC and Marshall tiptoed back down the hall. They stopped outside the door where the kids had gotten caught.

"The light's still on," KC whispered.

The room was quiet. When KC peeked around the door, she jumped.

The other men were gone, but the clone was still sitting in his chair. Now he was wide awake and tied with thick rope. His mouth was covered with tape. He was struggling to get free.

"We've got to get out of here," KC said.

She thought fast. "Could you come to my apartment?" she asked the president. "You can sleep in the guest room. My mom voted for you!"

The president looked around uneasily. "Yes, let's go."

"Wait! I sat under a bed for six hours for this." Marshall picked up a paper and pen off the table. "Mr. President, may I have your autograph?"

"Marshall!" KC groaned. "We're trying to escape here!"

But the president had already taken the pen and scrawled his signature.

Marshall beamed.

KC nearly fainted.

He had signed with his right hand!

7
Rescued

"Hey, thanks, Mr. President!" Marshall folded the paper and put it in his pocket.

KC stared at the president. Now she didn't know who was the president and who was the clone! If she helped the wrong one, who knew what would happen?

Feeling panicky, KC studied the two look-alikes. The man in the blue suit was right-handed. But KC knew the real president was left-handed.

"What's wrong, KC?" Marshall said. "You look like you swallowed a spider."

KC shook her head. "No, but I just thought of something." She smiled up at the president. "Sir, I need you to go back to the other room."

"Why?" the president asked. He looked confused.

"To buy us some time," she explained. "If anyone looks in, they'll know you're not there. But if you stuff pillows under the covers, they'll think you're in bed."

The president hesitated, then said, "Good idea. I'll be right back."

KC watched him leave the room. When he was gone, she grabbed Marshall. "Follow him!" she whispered. "As soon as he goes into that room, lock the door!"

Marshall's mouth fell open. "Huh? But why, KC?"

"Because he's the clone!" Then she pointed to the man tied in the chair. "This is the real president!"

The man in the chair mumbled behind his gag, nodding his head furiously.

"Now go!" KC shoved Marshall out the door. Marshall gave KC a look, but he hurried down the dark hall.

KC gently removed the tape from the struggling man's mouth.

"Water!" he gasped.

KC looked around the room. There was no water, but she grabbed a can of soda and held it to the man's lips.

After he took a few gulps, KC put the can down. Even in his pajamas and robe, this man looked exactly like the president.

But so did the other one! If she was wrong, she was making a terrible mistake!

Then KC had an idea. "How did you earn money to help your family?"

"I sold eggs to our neighbors," he said.

"How many brothers and sisters do you have?"

The man grinned. "There's Patricia, Trudy, Tommy, Roger, and the baby is Edward. That makes five!"

Anyone might know that, KC realized. "How many merit badges did you earn in the Scouts?" she asked.

The man blinked. "That was a long time ago. Ummm . . . twelve, why?"

Just then Marshall rushed back into the room. "He's locked in," he said. "I hope you're right about which one is which."

"Marshall, don't worry. This is the real President Thornton," KC said, grinning.

"Excuse me," the president said. "But could you untie me?"

"Oops, sorry, sir!" KC took out her knife and cut the ropes.

"Thanks!" The president stood up and rubbed his hands and ankles. "I expected the FBI or CIA, but you two look a little young for agents," he said. "Who are you? And what are you doing in the White House in the middle of the night?"

KC and Marshall introduced themselves and explained again.

The president laughed. "My mother always told me that being left-handed would make me stand out!"

Marshall pulled the folded paper out of his pocket. He looked at the clone's signature, then ripped it to pieces.

He picked up another piece of paper.

"Sir, could I please have your autograph?" he asked the real president.

"Sure, but can it wait? We need to get out of here." He glanced around the room.

"KC, did I hear you say something about your mother's apartment? Could we go there?"

KC nodded. "Won't Mom be surprised when she sees who I brought home!"

The president led KC and Marshall down the corridor. His slippers flip-flopped on the hard floor. He took them back to the kitchen, and stopped in front of the freezer.

"We're going into a freezer?" Marshall said.

The president smiled. "This one is special," he said. He twirled the combination lock a few times. The door popped open.

Suddenly KC heard voices.

"Sir, someone's coming!" she hissed to the president.

8
Secret Passageway

The president pulled KC and Marshall into the cold freezer.

"Hide!" he said as the door closed. He unscrewed a light bulb on the ceiling, then disappeared into the shadows.

Marshall jumped behind a stack of hamburger boxes. KC clambered over the boxes and crouched next to him.

The door to the freezer opened. Light fell onto the floor, and KC saw two shadows appear.

"Hey, Blinky," a man's voice said. "Someone left the lock open. Now's our chance to pig out!"

The two shadows came closer. Horror-struck, KC realized she could see her breath. She clapped both hands over her nose and mouth. Next to her, Marshall did the same.

One of the men stopped only inches from KC. She saw a pair of legs and dark leather shoes.

KC dared to look up from behind the boxes. The man standing there had been in the room with that awful guy in the white coat.

"Nah, it's all vegetables and meat," the man said. "No good stuff."

The feet turned and left. The door shut behind them. KC began to breathe again.

The president stepped out from behind some hanging beef. "Marshall, KC? Are you okay?" he asked.

"J-just a little c-cold," Marshall said.

"Come on," President Thornton said, walking to the rear of the chamber.

At the end of the freezer, the president shoved aside a few sides of beef. Behind them was a blank metal wall. Then the president said, "Zachary Thornton," in a clear voice. KC heard a whirring sound, and the wall slid sideways. In its place was a door.

The president punched in a code on the keypad by the door. The door opened. The kids followed him into a dark tunnel.

"This is so cool!" KC said.

"This secret passageway was built a long time ago," the president explained. "I think Teddy Roosevelt used it once."

"Where does it go?" Marshall asked, peering down the dim tunnel.

"You'll see, but let's hurry," the president said.

The tunnel sloped downhill for a while, then up. At the end, they climbed stairs leading to a door.

This one had a steel bar locking it from the inside. The president slid the bar out of its brackets. Behind the bar was a hole. The president reached into the hole and pulled out a tube.

"Periscope," he said, putting his eye to the tube. After a moment, he said, "All clear. Let's go!"

When the president pulled the door open, KC saw streetlights and cars whizzing by. "We're on Pennsylvania Avenue!" she said.

"That's right," the president said. "Just outside the White House fence."

They stepped through a narrow door onto grass. KC looked back. The door was hidden in a hollow concrete pillar that supported the gate to the White House grounds. When the president closed the door again, it disappeared.

"We can walk to my apartment," KC said. "It's not that far."

The president shook his head. "No, a taxi would be faster. I'm not exactly dressed for walking in February!"

He stepped to the curb, put two fingers into his mouth, and whistled loudly.

A taxi appeared and slowed down. The driver took one look, then sped away.

The president laughed. "I must look pretty strange," he said. His next whistle brought another cab. This one stopped.

"Where to?" the cabby said as the three

climbed into the backseat. She didn't seem to care about the man in his bathrobe and slippers.

"Five hundred 3rd Street," KC said.

"Got it!" The cabby pulled away with a squeal of tires. She looked in the rearview mirror. "Anyone ever tell you you look just like the president?" she asked. "You could be his clone!"

KC looked at Marshall and President Thornton. They all burst out laughing.

"What?" said the cabby. "What's so funny?"

Ten minutes later, the cab pulled up in front of KC and Marshall's building.

The president reached for his wallet. "Oops." His face turned red. "I forgot that I'm in my pajamas. Sorry, but I—I don't have any money on me."

KC rattled the money in her pack. "I do!" She counted out the fare and gave the driver a tip.

"Have a great night!" the cabdriver said before she zoomed away.

Marshall rang the bell on their building. A sleepy-eyed, yawning Donald came to the door. He woke right up when he saw KC and Marshall standing in the street.

Donald opened the door and let the three in. "What are you kids doing out at midnight?"

"Research for our reports," KC said, heading for the elevators.

"Oh, by the way," she added over her shoulder. "This is the president."

9
Slumber Party

"We're all going to my floor," KC told Donald in the elevator.

Donald stared at the president as the elevator rose. The president grinned and whistled "Yankee Doodle." Marshall yawned and scratched his mosquito bite.

At the fifth floor, they all .got out. "Good night, Donald," the president said.

Donald beamed. "Good night, Mr. President, your highness!"

KC used her key to let them into the apartment. Her mother was lying on the sofa reading a book.

"Katherine Christine, what are you

doing here?" she said. "I thought you were at Marshall's."

Then she noticed Marshall. "Why aren't you in bed? What's going on?"

And then KC's mom saw the man in the red pajamas and blue bathrobe.

"Mom, I'd like you to meet the president," KC said. "Mr. President, this is my mom, Lois Corcoran."

The president made a little bow. "Delighted, Ms. Corcoran. I owe my life to your daughter and Marshall."

KC's mother stood and removed her reading glasses. She stared at the man in front of her.

He was in his night clothes. He needed a shave. But he was smiling, the way he smiled in his posters.

"Oh my goodness!" KC's mother said,

looking down at her outfit. "I'm in my bathrobe!"

The president held out his hand. "So am I," he said. "So we're even."

KC scooted Lost and Found off a chair. "I hope you aren't allergic to cats," she said to the president.

"I love 'em," he said. "I have a cat in the White House for company." Then he looked at KC's mother. "May I use the phone? I need to alert the CIA that we have some scoundrels in the White House."

"You can use the one in the kitchen," KC's mom said, pointing the way.

While the president was gone, KC told her mother the whole story.

"Spiders?" KC's mom asked.

"Well, it worked," KC said.

"You really released spiders in the

Lincoln bedroom?" her mother said as the president walked back into the room.

Marshall looked up at the president. "Will I get in trouble?"

The president laughed. "Not at all! You two and those spiders are heroes!"

"How did it happen?" KC asked the president. "I mean, how did you get cloned?"

The president pulled up a chair. "It was a very clever plan, actually," he said. "A scientist named Dr. Jenks figured out a way to clone humans. He and his greedy friends spent years perfecting the process. They learned how to make an adult clone from a hair sample. That's what they did with me."

Lost and Found jumped into the president's lap. They began purring.

The president continued. "When my clone was ready, Dr. Jenks set up a meeting to discuss his cloning ideas. I listened to what he had to say, but I told him I was against the cloning of humans."

The president shook his head. "We were having coffee. It was late. My staff had gone home. The last thing I remember is Dr. Jenks saying good night and shaking my hand."

He looked at his listeners. "He must have drugged my coffee and ordered the clone to give the real guards the night off. That was yesterday. I woke up this morning in the basement dressed like this."

"They must have given your suit to the clone," KC said. "You looked drugged when Marsh and I first saw you."

The president nodded. "The drug wore

off, but I pretended I was still asleep so I could listen. With me out of the way, the clone could lie to the world and announce the new cloning policy. Dr. Jenks and his team would make millions cloning humans!"

"But that would be awful!" Marshall cried. "We have to stop them!"

"Don't worry, Marshall," the president said. "The CIA is on the case."

While the president chatted with her mom, KC closed her eyes and dozed off in her chair. She dreamed about Cindy Sparks announcing the news tomorrow:

Local fourth-grade heroes rescue President Thornton and save the world!

10
Spiders Rule

KC peeked out the window in the Oval Office. "Look, Marsh, I see Mr. Alubicki! He's in the fourth row with our class! And there's my mom and your parents!"

Marshall joined her at the window. "Our whole school is out there! Cool!"

It was a week later. KC and Marshall had received A's for their reports. To Marshall's surprise, President Hoover had collected bugs when he was a kid!

But the big surprise was the phone call from the president's secretary. KC and Marshall were invited to the White House. They were going to receive a special award for rescuing the president!

The door opened, and the president walked in. He was carrying two small jewelry boxes. "We'll be going out to the lawn in a few minutes," he said. "But first, I wanted to thank you two in private."

KC blushed.

Marshall noticed a spider crawling down a wall. "Hey, I wonder if that's one of mine!" he said.

The president smiled. "Could be. But don't worry, it'll be safe here. I've issued a memo to all staff. Starting now, spiders are special guests in the White House."

The president handed Marshall and KC each a box. "Please open them," he said.

KC lifted the fancy lid. On a layer of red velvet, she found a satin ribbon and a round gold medal.

"It's beautiful!" she said.

"This is real g-gold!" Marshall cried.

"Read what's inscribed on the medals," the president said.

KC read hers. In a circle were the words: *To KC Corcoran for Bravery*. She flipped her medal over. On the back was an engraving of a spider.

"This is so cool!" Marshall said, hanging his medal around his neck.

"I have one, too." The president unbuttoned his suit jacket and held up his medal. "Mine is just like yours. But it has both your names on the front."

"And a spider on the back?" Marshall asked.

The president grinned at Marshall. "Yep. A spider on the back."

A man peeked in the door. "Mr.

President, they're ready for you outside."

KC gasped when she saw the man's face. "It's the clone!"

The president smiled. "Yes, I interviewed him when Dr. Jenks was arrested. My clone is really a nice guy. He never understood what Dr. Jenks was up to. I've decided to keep him on my staff."

"But won't everyone get confused?" KC asked.

The president winked. "That might be fun," he said. "I've always wanted to have a twin."

He beckoned to the man standing by the door. "By the way," he said to KC and Marshall, "we've given him a special name."

The clone walked over. He proudly showed the kids his name tag. It said, MR. CASEY MARSHALL.

"Wow!" KC said. "We have a clone named after us, Marsh!"

Casey Marshall smiled. "I'll tell them you'll be out in a minute, sir." He left and closed the door behind him.

Marshall dug a paper from his pocket. He held it out to the president.

"You said you'd give me your autograph, Mr. President."

The president took the paper. "You're right, I did promise."

He walked to his desk, picked up a pen, and signed "Zachary Thornton."

· With his left hand.

This is the end of

WHO CLONED THE PRESIDENT?

Turn the page to read

KIDNAPPED AT THE CAPITAL.

KIDNAPPED
AT THE CAPITAL

by **Ron Roy**
illustrated by **Liza Woodruff**

1
Vanished

"Come and eat, kitties!" KC Corcoran called out. She filled a bowl with cat food and set it on the floor. Lost and Found, her two kittens, came sliding around the corner when they heard the sound.

Marshall Li, KC's best friend, poured water into another bowl.

"We have to leave soon," KC's mom said. Lois Corcoran held up an engraved invitation. "It's almost ten o'clock. The president is meeting us outside the Air and Space Museum in half an hour."

"Do you think Casey Marshall will be there, too?" KC asked.

"I doubt it," her mother said, looking for her keys. "The president doesn't want the public to know he has a clone."

The President of the United States had invited KC, her mom, and Marshall to the Cherry Blossom Festival. Each April, this celebration was held on the National Mall in Washington, D.C. Thousands of people came out to enjoy the museums and the beautiful pink cherry blossoms.

KC and Marshall had become friends with President Zachary Thornton when they'd rescued him from evil scientists. The scientists had cloned the president, hoping to use the clone for their own purposes.

But KC and Marshall had saved the president, and the president had saved the clone. Now the clone—named Casey

Marshall after KC and Marshall—lived in the White House.

"Do I have time to run downstairs and feed Spike?" Marshall asked.

Marshall lived in an apartment two floors below KC. He was staying with the Corcorans while his parents were away buying antiques for his mom's shop.

"If you hurry," KC's mom said. "We'll meet you in the lobby in five minutes."

KC watched Marshall dash out the door. Spike was his pet tarantula. KC shuddered, thinking of all those hairy legs.

Five minutes later, KC, her mom, and Marshall met in the lobby.

"Say hi to the president for me," said Donald. He held the door open. Donald was the building manager, and he was also their friend.

The National Mall was a short walk from the apartments. They passed the Capitol building, then cut through the Botanic Gardens. The cherry trees that lined the grassy strip were in full bloom. Everywhere KC looked, people were going in and out of the museums and other buildings on the National Mall.

Kids zoomed around on roller blades. Joggers dodged baby strollers. Vendors stood behind carts selling food, T-shirts, and Washington, D.C. souvenirs.

"There he is!" Marshall pointed to a group of people next to the National Air and Space Museum. In the center of the group stood the president, wearing khaki pants, a blue sweater, and a baseball cap. All around him were secret service agents in dark suits. The president chatted and shook hands with everyone who came up to him.

"Isn't it great," KC's mom said, "that President Thornton gets out to meet the people who elected him?"

The president looked up and waved at KC, her mom, and Marshall. The secret service agents made an opening for them through the crowd.

"Hi! Thanks for coming," the president said when they reached him. "Aren't the cherry blossoms beautiful?"

"Lovely!" KC's mom said. She picked a blossom from a tree and tucked it in her hair. "Thank you for inviting us, Mr. President."

"The cherry trees are so pink!" KC said. "I feel like I'm walking through strawberry ice cream!"

"Mmmm, ice cream!" said Marshall.

"Now there's a good idea," KC's mom said. "Would you like to get some?" She dug in her purse, then handed KC a five-dollar bill.

KC and Marshall went looking for an ice cream cart. "President Thornton is so cool," Marshall said. "Maybe I'll run for president some day."

"I thought you wanted to be a bug scientist," KC reminded her friend.

Marshall shrugged. "I can always be an entomologist in my spare time."

"I don't think presidents get much time for hobbies," KC said.

"That's lousy," Marshall said. "If I can't bring my spiders, I'm not gonna be president!"

KC laughed. "I'd vote for you, but only

if you made me the TV anchor for the White House."

Marshall spotted a group of food carts in front of the Smithsonian castle. He and KC walked over to a teenager selling ice cream cones.

"What'll it be?" the teenager asked.

"A cherry and pistachio cone, please," Marshall told the kid. "One scoop of each, with the pistachio on top."

"Awesome," the teenager said. "Looks like Christmas."

"I'll have butter crunch," KC said. "One scoop."

She paid with her mom's money, then they began walking back toward the Air and Space Museum.

"I wonder who planted all these cherry trees," Marshall said.

"Johnny Cherryseed," KC said, licking her cone.

Marshall laughed. A few minutes later, they reached the spot where they'd left KC's mom. KC stood on her tiptoes. She tried to spot her mother and the president over the other people.

"Do you see them anywhere?" she asked Marshall.

"Nope, but wait a sec." Marshall climbed onto the seat of a bench. He craned his neck, looking in all directions. "I don't see them," he said.

"That's funny," KC said. She joined Marshall on the bench. "There aren't any secret service guys, either."

"They've gotta be around here," Marshall said. "Maybe your mom and the president went for a walk."

KC shook her head. She was beginning to feel worried. "Mom wouldn't take off without letting me know," she said.

KC's ice cream cone dripped on her hand, but she ignored it. With her heart beating fast, she searched the crowd. Nowhere did she see a man in a baseball cap and a woman wearing a purple dress.

President Thornton and her mother had vanished!

2
Top Secret

"Maybe they went into one of the buildings," Marshall suggested.

KC gazed up and down the Mall. The Washington Monument was at one end, and the Capitol stood at the other. Museums lined either side of the long, grassy lawn.

KC shook her head. "Marshall, my mom has this rule—if one of us changes a plan, we tell the other one. She reminds me all the time." KC hopped off the bench and threw her unfinished cone into a trash can. "I think something happened to her and President Thornton!"

"There's something else your mom tells you all the time," Marshall said, still working on his cone. "Don't jump to conclusions."

"I'm not jumping to anything!" KC said. "She was supposed to be here, and she's not. Wouldn't you worry if your mom disappeared into thin air?"

"Okay, sure I would," Marshall agreed. "So what should we do?"

"Let's look around the Mall," KC said. "They have to be somewhere."

KC and Marshall walked the length of the Mall and back. Crowds of people were out, enjoying the sunshine and the cherry blossoms. Twenty minutes later, KC and Marshall were in front of the Air and Space Museum again.

"Something has happened to them,"

KC told Marshall. Her stomach felt jumpy, like she was about to be sick. "I think we should go home. I'm sure Mom will call me."

They retraced their steps toward home. KC studied the people around her. She kept hoping to spot that purple dress.

Back at their building, Donald held the door open for them. "Have you seen my mother?" KC asked him.

Donald looked puzzled. "Weren't you all together?"

"We were," KC explained. "But then my mom and the president disappeared. Did she come here?"

Donald shook his head. "I haven't seen her since you guys left," he said. "And I've been in the lobby the whole time."

KC had tears in her eyes. "What could

have happened to them?" she said.

Donald put a hand on her shoulder. "If Lois is with the president, I'm sure she's fine," he said. "He's always surrounded by his secret service agents."

KC nodded. "But we should go upstairs in case she calls."

"Good idea," Donald said. "I'll bet your phone rings in five minutes!" He walked with them to the elevator and took them up to the fifth floor.

KC let them in with her key. She prayed the phone would be ringing. But the apartment was silent. Lost and Found were asleep on the sofa.

KC switched on the TV and used the remote to find the local news. Standing in front of the TV, she surfed between channels. "Nothing," she muttered.

"What are you looking for?" Marshall asked. He sat next to the kittens and stroked their soft fur.

"I don't know," KC said. "But if something happened to the president, it'd be on the news, right?"

Marshall smiled at his friend. "Of course it would," he said. "So that means nothing bad has happened."

"I guess," KC said. "But Mom would never just go off somewhere!"

KC continued to surf, hitting all the news channels. Finally she gave up and punched the OFF button.

She flopped down on the floor. *Everything's going to be all right,* she told herself. But still she felt scared. And sad.

KC thought about her father down in Florida. Maybe she should call him. But she couldn't—she had to leave the phone line open.

As if by magic, the phone rang.

KC leaped up to answer it with her fingers crossed. Marshall ran into the kitchen and picked up the extension.

KC reached the phone on the second ring. "Mom?" she said.

"KC? This is the president," a familiar voice answered.

To KC, it sounded as if he had a stuffy nose. She was suspicious. The president didn't have a cold when she saw him a little while ago! "Are you with my mom?" she asked.

"No, I'm not," the president said. "That's why I called."

"Where is she?" KC almost yelled. "She was with you!"

"No, she was with Casey Marshall," the president said. "I came down with a cold, so I sent Casey to meet you instead."

"But where are they?" KC asked. "Marshall and I went to get ice cream and they disappeared!"

"KC, I'd rather talk to you about this in person," President Thornton said. "I'm sending a car to pick up you and Marshall and bring you to the White House. I'll explain everything when I see you."

"Is my mom all right?" KC asked. "Shouldn't I stay here in case she calls?"

There was silence on the phone. "I can only say I think she's fine," the president said finally. "But she isn't in a position to call you."

Now KC was really worried. Her hands felt hot and cold at the same time.

"The car will be there in five minutes," the president continued. "Will you be downstairs?"

KC gulped. "Yes, sir."

"Before you hang up," the president added, "have you told anyone else about what happened?"

"Only Donald," KC said.

There was a pause. "Okay, but please ask him not to say a word," the president warned. "This is top secret!"

3
Kidnapped

Instead of waiting for the elevator, KC and Marshall ran down the fire stairs. Donald looked surprised to see them. "Did your mom call?" he asked hopefully.

"No, but the president did," KC said. "We're going to the White House. He says my mom is all right. And he said, 'Tell Donald not to say a word to anyone!' "

Donald's face turned pink. "The president knows my name?"

KC nodded. "He wanted me to tell you it's top secret!"

"Please let the president know that these lips are sealed!" Donald closed an invisible zipper over his mouth.

"I think the car's here," Marshall said, pointing through the glass door.

"Oh my," Donald said.

The car was long and black. A small American flag flew from the antenna.

KC and Marshall hurried to the car just as the driver stepped out. Wearing a suit and tie, he walked smartly around the car and opened the rear door. "I'm here to take KC and Marshall to the White House. Is that you?"

KC looked at the man. He was tall with very short hair. His eyes were hidden behind dark glasses. KC suddenly felt wary. *Is this guy really from the White House?* she wondered. She wasn't sure she wanted to get into the car.

KC decided to test him. "The president

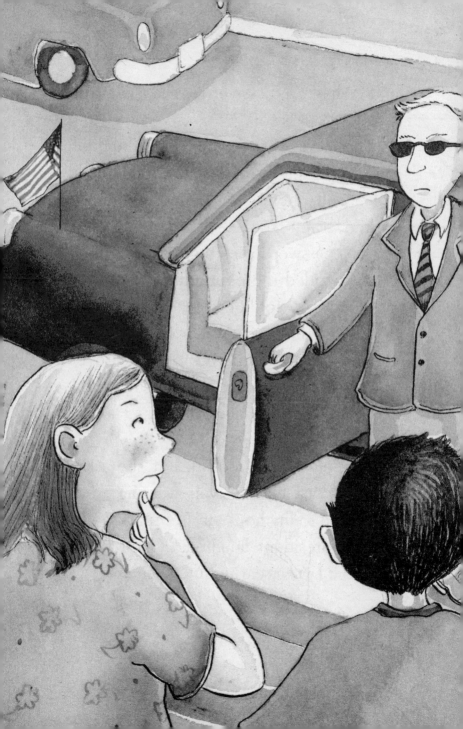

and I have a password," she said. "So what's the password?"

The man hesitated, then shut the door. From a pocket inside his jacket, he pulled out a cell phone. He dialed a number, waited, then spoke. "The young lady wants a password, sir," the man said.

He handed the phone to KC. "It's the president," he told her.

KC put the phone to her ear. "Hi, KC," the president said. "You are wise to be cautious. I should have thought of the password idea myself. How can I assure you that I'm the president?"

KC felt a little foolish, but she asked anyway. "What were you wearing when you came to my house in February?"

The president laughed. "Good thinking, KC. I was wearing my pajamas."

KC smiled. "Thanks, sir! See you in a few minutes." She handed the cell phone to the driver.

He was grinning. "Satisfied?"

"Yes, thank you."

He opened the door again and KC and Marshall stepped inside.

The car zoomed down Constitution Avenue, then turned through the White House gates. The driver made two more turns and stopped. "The president's private entrance," he said. He came around and opened their door. "Someone will come for you in a minute."

The driver got back into the car and drove away.

Marshall nudged KC's arm. "Look," he said.

A marine marched over to them. His

uniform was crisply pressed and his black shoes sparkled. "The president is waiting for you," he said. "Will you follow me, please?"

He turned and marched away. KC and Marshall hurried to keep up. They went through a door, down a hallway with thick carpeting, and up an elevator.

Finally they came to a wide door. The marine knocked twice with his white-gloved knuckles.

"Yes," a voice said.

The marine opened the door and stepped aside so KC and Marshall could enter.

The president was sitting in a chair. He was wearing a gray sweatshirt and baggy pants. A fluffy orange cat sat in his lap.

"Thank you, sergeant," the president

said. He looked pale, and the rims of his eyes were red and puffy.

The marine saluted, stepped back, and closed the door.

"Hi, you two," the president said. His voice was hoarse. "Come on in." Then he sneezed.

A tall woman came into the room. "Hello, I'm Vice President Mary Kincaid," she said. "Won't you have a seat?"

KC and Marshall shook her hand, then sat on a sofa.

"President Thornton hasn't much of a voice right now," the vice president said. "So I'll tell you what we know. At ten forty-two this morning, the president's secret service men reported that someone had kidnapped President Thornton."

"Obviously, they were wrong," the

president said. "For security reasons, the secret service agents hadn't been told that I sent Casey Marshall to meet you."

"Unfortunately, they took KC's mother along with Casey," Mary Kincaid said.

KC swallowed the lump in her throat. "Does anyone know where they are?"

Mary Kincaid shook her head. "No, but we've received a ransom letter by fax. The message assures us that Casey and your mother are safe and well. The kidnappers promise to let them go as soon as the White House meets their demands."

The room was silent, except for the cat's purring.

"What do they want?" Marshall asked.

"What they asked for," the president said, "is the International Space Station."

4

The Search Begins

The vice president went on. "They want to go aboard the space station," she stated. "They want to take it over."

"But aren't there astronauts living on it now?" Marshall asked.

The president nodded. "Yes, ours as well as astronauts from other countries."

"So what happens to them if the kidnappers get onboard?" KC asked.

"Everyone will have to leave," the vice president said. "Apparently, the kidnappers want to be the only folks up there."

"What are they gonna do with a space station?" Marshall asked.

"That is the question, isn't it?" the president said. "But more importantly, I want you to know, KC, that we're doing everything we can to get your mother back."

"The FBI and others are searching this town," Mary Kincaid informed the kids. "Every street has a roadblock. Every building is being searched. The bus and train stations and airport are being checked. SWAT team helicopters are in the air right now. We'll find your mother."

KC swallowed back her tears. "Thank you," she said.

"Please be my guest in the White House while we wait this out," the president offered. "You too, Marshall."

"Thank you, sir," KC said. "But is it okay if I go home and feed my cats?"

"I'll have a car take you," Mary Kincaid

said. She reached for the telephone.

"Um, we'd rather walk," KC said. "It's not far."

The president scooted the cat off his lap and stood up. "Try not to worry," he said. "We have a hundred of our best people looking for Casey and your mother. I know we'll get them back soon."

He leaned over the desk and scribbled something on a small pad. "Here's my private phone number," he said, handing the top sheet to KC. "Call if you need anything at all."

The president sneezed again. He wiped his nose with a handkerchief. "I'm going back to bed. Mary, will you show KC and Marshall the way out?"

"Of course. Come on, kids."

Mary Kincaid escorted them to the

hall, then signaled to the marine who was waiting. "Please take KC and Marshall to the special exit," she said.

"Yes, Madam Vice President," he said.

KC and Marshall followed the marine down the hall, into the elevator, and out the private exit. He gave them a salute as they headed toward Pennsylvania Avenue.

As soon as the marine was out of sight, Marshall stopped KC. "Okay, you're up to something," Marshall said. "What's this about feeding your cats? I saw you fill up their food bowl an hour ago."

"I know," KC said. "We're not going home."

"We're not? Where are we going?"

"To look for my mother." KC started walking again. Marshall hurried to keep up with her.

"But the president told us a hundred guys are already looking," Marshall said.

"And women, too, Marshall," KC said. "Not all FBI agents are men, you know."

"Okay, sue me," Marshall said. "But how are we supposed to find your mom and Casey?"

They were approaching the Museum of Natural History. Across Madison Drive, they could see the flags flying over the Smithsonian castle.

"By looking for clues," KC said.

"How can two kids . . ." Marshall stopped and gave KC a long look. KC didn't meet his eyes. "Okay," he said after a minute. "We'll do whatever you want. Where should we start?"

They ended up on Constitution Avenue, near the Washington Monument.

"Let's start here," KC said. "Then we can walk toward the Capitol. And check every building—inside and out!"

"There are a lot of buildings," Marshall said.

"So we'll split up," KC said: "We'll meet in about half an hour in front of the Air and Space Museum."

They decided that Marshall would take the buildings on the north side of the Mall. KC would check the south side. She started in the Washington Monument. From there she went to a couple of art museums, then the Smithsonian castle.

KC worked her way along the Mall, looking everywhere she could think of. She searched the sculpture gardens and the carousel. She went in every museum. Luckily, they all had free admission.

KC was hot, tired, and sweaty when she finally met Marshall by the Air and Space Museum. "Any luck?" she asked.

"No," he said. "But in the Natural History Museum, I saw a tarantula even bigger than Spike!"

KC sat down on the steps outside the space museum. "Do you want to do this one, or should I?"

"Do you really think we'll find them?" Marshall commented. "I mean—"

"We can't just go back to the White House and do nothing, Marsh," KC said. "Someone took my mom and I'm getting her back . . . even if I have to search every inch of Washington, D.C.!"

5
Space Mission

"Okay, okay, we'll check in here," said Marshall. He shoved open the door of the museum. KC and Marshall were greeted by cool air and a crowd of people.

The room they entered was cavernous. The walls were glass, letting in the sunlight. Airplanes, spacecraft, missiles, rockets, and other things were on display. The Wright brothers' 1903 Flyer was there, along with the Spirit of St. Louis. Some displays were roped off to keep visitors from touching anything.

"Okay," KC said, "let's ask people if they saw the president."

They split up. KC approached a man with two little boys. They were looking at an exhibit about hot air balloons.

"Excuse me," KC said. "But have you seen the president today?"

"What president?" the man asked.

"Of the United States," KC said. "President Thornton."

"Cool!" one of the boys said. "The president is here!"

The man looked at KC. "Is he really?"

KC sighed. "I don't know," she said. "Did you see him? He was with a woman in a purple dress."

The man shook his head. "Sorry, I was too busy watching my kids."

KC asked other people. She saw Marshall doing the same thing. Everyone shook their heads, no.

She walked across the room to join Marshall. "No luck, huh?" she asked.

"Nope. But I talked to one guy who shook his hand outside."

"That was before they disappeared." KC glanced at a wide set of stairs. A small sign posted by the steps read:

More Displays on Second Floor

"Come on," she said, starting up the staircase. At the top, she stopped to watch the crowd in the main gallery.

Marshall bumped shoulders with KC. "Let's keep looking," he said.

They checked out the second floor displays. They saw war planes and an exhibit about exploring the planets. Marshall stopped in front of a meteorite found in Antarctica.

They came to an open doorway with a sign on a pedestal that read:

CAUTION—WET FLOOR
APOLLO 11
LUNAR MODULE
EXHIBIT CLOSED TODAY

A red velvet rope blocked the entrance. A man in a gray uniform was standing on the shiny floor just inside the room.

"This is so neat," Marshall said. He leaned over the rope for a better look.

In the center of the room stood the lunar module of Apollo 11, the first space-craft to land on the moon. Under Apollo 11, a circle of dust and rocks represented the moon's surface. Twenty feet above, two fake astronauts wearing space suits

CAUTION

hung from cables attached to the ceiling.

"Excuse me," the man said. He was tall and thin, with a deep voice. "This exhibit is closed today."

"Sorry," Marshall said.

For about the hundredth time, KC asked, "Have you seen the president in here today? He was with my mother. She was wearing a purple dress."

The man frowned and shook his head. "I'm too busy to notice who comes in and out," he said. He left them at the door and walked toward the module.

Near the Apollo 11, the man stooped and picked something off the floor. He stared at it, glanced back at KC and Marshall, then quickly shoved it in his pocket.

"Did you see that?" KC whispered.

"What?" asked Marshall.

"There was a cherry blossom on the floor," KC said. "That janitor put it in his pocket."

Marshall shrugged. "So? There are about a million cherry blossoms all over Washington."

"But this floor has just been cleaned. No one is allowed to walk on it. So how did a cherry blossom get there?"

KC stared at the man in the gray uniform. "And besides, my mother had one in her hair," she said.

6
Flowers on the Moon

"What are you saying?" Marshall asked.

"Marsh, my mom had a pink flower in her hair when she disappeared. And there was a cherry blossom on the floor where there shouldn't be one. It doesn't make sense."

"So maybe somebody dropped it," Marshall said.

"Yes, and maybe that somebody was my mother!" KC said. "It's the first clue we've found, Marsh. Come on, let's search the rest of this place. Maybe my mother is here!"

They walked from exhibit to exhibit.

They looked in every room on the second floor, but didn't discover anything new. Marshall flopped down on a bench. KC joined him. They didn't talk.

KC sat and stared at the floor. Suddenly two pairs of feet stepped into her line of sight.

"Did you find your mother?" a familiar voice asked.

KC looked up. The feet belonged to the tall janitor they had spoken to before. Another man was with him, dressed in a similar uniform. The second janitor was short and round, with little eyes that kept blinking.

A tingly feeling crept up KC's spine. Something was wrong here. She took a deep breath and smiled at the two men. "No, but my mom is supposed to meet me here later," she said. "We're gonna hang out until then."

"Okay," the taller man said. "Just stay off the wet floor."

"Sure thing," KC said. As the men walked away, she grabbed Marshall's arm.

"What do you mean your mom's supposed to meet us here?" Marshall hissed. "What's going on?"

"Did you see the shoes those guys are wearing?" KC asked.

Marshall started to turn around.

"No, don't look now!" KC said, grabbing him again.

"How can I see their shoes if you won't let me look?" Marshall asked.

"They're wearing dress-up shoes," KC said.

Marshall stared at KC. "What do you

mean, 'dress-up' shoes? I don't get it."

"Marsh, if you were mopping floors, would you wear expensive shoes?" KC asked. "The janitor at school wears work boots or old sneakers. But those two guys are wearing good shoes, real shiny."

"And that means . . . ?"

"It means maybe they're pretending to be janitors, Marsh."

"Why would anyone pretend to be a janitor?" Marshall asked.

"That's what we need to find out," KC said. "Come on."

KC checked over her shoulder to make sure they weren't being watched. Then she led Marshall back to the Apollo 11 display.

They stopped at the red rope. KC bent down and touched the floor. "The janitor just said it was wet. But it's dry," she mumbled. "So why is the exhibit still closed?"

KC and Marshall gazed past the velvet rope. Nothing had changed. The Apollo 11 stood in the middle of the room with its spindly legs stuck in powdery "moon dust." The two fake astronauts hung from above.

Suddenly Marshall jumped. "Huh?" he said. He blinked his eyes and stared at the hanging space suits. "Did you see that?"

"See what?" KC asked.

"You're not gonna believe this," said Marshall, "but I swear one of those space suit guys just moved."

KC looked up at the hanging space suits. "Stop joking around, Marshall," she said. "They're fake." Feeling an itch, she rubbed her nose.

When she looked up again, one of the astronauts was rubbing its face mask.

"There it is again!" Marshall said. "It moved!"

"I saw it!" KC shouted. She wiggled her fingers.

The astronaut wiggled its fingers.

KC knocked the velvet rope out of the way. She sprinted into the room and waved her arms frantically at the two space suits.

Slowly, one of them waved back at her.

7

Run and Hide

"Mom!" KC screamed up at the two space suits.

"Is it them?" Marshall asked from behind KC.

"It has to be!" KC said to Marshall. "Help me figure out a way to get them down!"

"Hey, you kids! Get away from that exhibit!" a voice rang out.

"Uh-oh," Marshall muttered.

The tall janitor entered the room. "What do you think you're doing?" he asked.

The man walked slowly toward KC and

Marshall. His eyes were squinty, and his long hands curled into fists.

KC took a deep breath. Then she bent over and picked up a small rock from the pile beneath the Apollo 11.

"Thank goodness you're here!" she said, holding out the rock. "Look, I've found a clue about the missing president!"

The man's frown turned to a look of puzzlement. He stared first at the rock in KC's hand, then turned his eyes upward toward the two space suits.

Which is exactly what KC hoped he would do.

"Run!" she screamed at Marshall.

The man reached for KC, but she dodged away. He positioned himself in front of the exit with an evil sneer on his face.

Marshall charged right for the man, as if

he was going to knock him over. But at the last second, Marshall flung himself down like a kid sliding into second base. He slid across the floor, slipping right between the man's long legs. When the man whirled around, KC darted past him.

KC and Marshall dashed down the stairs and out into the crowded main room.

"This way!" KC said, running over to a group of kids. She and Marshall wiggled to the front, right next to one of the chaperones.

Safe for now, KC caught her breath. She was still holding the rock, so she slipped it into her pocket. Cautiously, she looked over her shoulder.

The man glared back at her. His face was red and his eyes flashed with anger.

She saw him start walking toward the school group.

KC forced herself to stay calm and think. He wouldn't dare grab two kids in front of all these people, would he?

She decided he would. He'd just say that these children had stolen a moon rock from the Apollo exhibit. Then he'd take her and Marshall away and . . .

KC felt herself begin to panic. The man was coming closer. Should she yell out that this guy had kidnapped the president and hidden him in a space suit?

KC realized that nobody would believe her. They'd laugh or think she was lying to get out of trouble.

Marshall tugged on her arm. "KC, that guy's getting closer! What are we gonna do?"

KC made a decision. "We have to split up," she whispered, slipping Marshall the phone number. "You call the president. Tell him we found my mom and Casey. I'll try to get that guy to follow me."

Marshall hesitated. "Okay. Be careful, KC."

"I will," KC said. "Tell the president to send the SWAT team!" Then KC turned to the group's chaperone.

"Excuse me!" she said loudly. Out of the corner of her eye, KC saw the janitor stop and watch her. "Would you please take me to the bathroom?" she asked the chaperone.

The woman looked puzzled. "You're not part of my group, are you?" she asked.

"I know," KC said. "I lost my group, and I really have to go!"

"Of course I'll take you," the chaperone said. "It's this way." She took KC's hand and they headed away from the group.

KC glanced over her shoulder. Yes! The man was following her, not Marshall. She shuddered. He reminded her of a lion stalking its prey.

The chaperone paused in front of the bathrooms. Before KC could thank her and dash inside, the man put his hand on her shoulder.

"I'm sorry," he said to the chaperone. "This girl stole something from the Apollo exhibit." He held out his large hand. "May I have it, please?"

KC gulped and looked down. The rock she had picked up made a bulge in her pocket. She slowly took it out and gave it to the man.

The kind chaperone was staring at her. KC felt her face turn red.

"Now, if you'll come with me," the man said, "I'm taking you to security."

"Is that necessary?" the chaperone asked, smiling at the fake janitor. "She's returned the rock."

The man glared at the woman. "Stealing moon rocks is a federal offense!" he said. He put his hand on KC's shoulder and led her away.

"Where are you taking me?" KC demanded.

"Quiet," the man said. His hand felt as if it were burning KC's shoulder.

They came to the Apollo exhibit. The wet floor sign was gone, and the door was closed. The man pulled a key from his pocket and inserted it into the lock. He shoved KC into the room and closed the door behind them.

The other janitor stood there with his hands on his hips and a smirk on his face. His piggy eyes blinked rapidly. When he moved aside, KC almost fainted.

Marshall was sitting on the floor beneath the Apollo. His hands and feet were bound, and a red cloth was tied around his mouth.

8
Doomed

KC felt sick. Marshall stared back at her, mumbling something through his gag.

The tall man laughed. "Waldo here caught your little friend trying to make a phone call," he said.

He held up the slip of paper with the president's phone number. He ripped it into pieces and let them fall from his hands.

KC watched the bits of paper flutter to the floor by her feet. Calling the president had been their only chance. Now no one knew where they were. She and her mom, Marshall and Casey were doomed.

With tears in her eyes, KC looked up at the two space suits. One of them waved down at her.

"Very clever of you to have found them," the tall janitor said. "What tipped you off?"

KC wiped her nose with her sleeve. "The flower you picked up," KC told the man. "My mother dropped it there."

"Well," the man said, "like Hansel and Gretel's bread crumbs, the flower won't do your mother and the president any good."

"I hope you go to jail for a million years!" KC shouted.

The man snorted. "First they have to catch me. And where I'm going, they won't."

"Please let my mother down," KC

pleaded. "She gets dizzy from heights."

"What're we gonna do with them, Chip?" Waldo asked, ignoring KC. "We don't need four hostages."

Chip laughed. "We'll take them with us," he said. "With the president as our guest, nobody will bother us. I doubt anyone will try to destroy the space station with the President of the United States aboard!"

He glanced down at the kids. "But I have other plans for the woman and these two. Once we get to the space station, they'll be taking a space walk of their own. Only they won't be wearing space suits!"

The two men high-fived each other.

"You'll never get away with this!" KC said.

"Wrong," Chip said, holding up his cell

phone. "We've just been notified that we're cleared to get on the shuttle. Ralphy's on his way with the helicopter."

"Prepare to say bye-bye to Earth," Waldo said. He pulled a rope from his pocket and began tying KC's hands behind her back.

Suddenly he stopped and looked up. His tiny eyes blinked. "Did you hear that?" he asked Chip. "I think it's our ride."

The taller man smiled. "Yes, it's the chopper. Next stop, Florida."

Waldo finished tying up KC, then sat her next to Marshall. He and Chip walked away and stood by the closed door.

KC moved closer to Marshall, directly under her mother. "I'm sorry," she whispered. She thought about her father again, and her kittens. She wondered if Marshall was thinking about his family.

Suddenly three things happened at once—a terrific crashing noise made KC jump, the door burst open, and two men thundered into the room. They were followed by about ten men and women wearing SWAT team uniforms.

One of the women strode up to Chip and Waldo, who were cringing in a corner. "Hands out and mouths shut," she said. She snapped her fingers at one of her team members. "Wrap these two to go."

"With pleasure," the man said as he clicked handcuffs onto the kidnappers' wrists.

The woman strode over and knelt in front of KC and Marshall. "Are you okay?" she asked.

KC couldn't find her voice. She nodded instead.

"Are you Marshall?" the woman asked, untying his gag.

Marshall licked his lips, then grinned and said, "Yeah. What took you so long?"

"Long?" The woman looked at her watch. "You called only ten minutes ago."

KC stared at Marshall. "You called the president's number?"

"Yup. That goon grabbed me right after I hung up." Marshall grinned. "I let him think he got me before I made the phone call."

"Marshall Li, I'm mad at you!" KC said. "Why didn't you tell me you made the call?"

Marshall held up the red cloth. "I was gagged, remember?"

9
1600 Pennsylvania Avenue

The next morning, another black car picked up KC, her mom, and Marshall. They were driven to the White House and escorted to President Thornton's private residence. They found him sipping a glass of orange juice.

"Good morning," the president said when they entered. He looked much better. His eyes were still a little red, but he wasn't sneezing anymore.

"How are you feeling?" KC asked.

"Much improved, now that I know you're all safe."

"So where's Casey?" Marshall asked.

"Poor guy, I sent him on a vacation. He's in disguise, so no one will mistake him for me this time." President Thornton looked at KC's mom. "Ms. Corcoran, please accept my—"

KC's mom interrupted. "Please call me Lois, Mr. President."

The president smiled. "Okay, if you'll call me Zach." He cleared his throat and started again. "Lois, I'm so sorry I didn't come to meet you yesterday."

Lois nodded. "At first I thought Casey was joking," she said. "He asked the secret service men to give us a moment alone and started to explain. That's when those two men grabbed us."

"Who were they, anyway?" KC asked.

The president took a sip of juice. "Chip Hornbeck and Waldo Weeks are disgruntled astronauts," he said. "They were kicked out of NASA two years ago, and never got to go into space. They were unhappy and decided to get revenge."

"So they were only pretending to be janitors, right?" KC asked.

The president nodded. "Because they were astronauts, they knew all the off-limit places in the Air and Space Museum."

Just then Marshall's stomach growled.

"Well, I guess we'd better eat," said the president. "Please sit down, everyone."

They all sat and began passing platters of scrambled eggs, fruit, and bagels. The president's cat sat by his feet and meowed loudly.

"Sorry, George," the president said. He dropped a cherry onto the carpet.

"Why did you name him George?" Marshall asked.

The president grinned. "For the first president," he said. "And you know how he liked cherries!"

George held the cherry with his front paws and took delicate bites.

"Anyway," the president continued, "Chip and Waldo will be in jail for quite a long time."

"There was a third man," KC's mom said. "He was waiting inside the rear door of the museum. He had rags dipped in something awful that they put over our faces. When I woke up, they were putting me in that space suit!"

"Ralphy Bird," the president said. "We've already got him. He was caught in a helicopter, hovering over the museum."

"Was it scary hanging up there?" Marshall asked KC's mom.

"Oh, honey, you have no idea!" she said. "When I saw you two walk into the room, I thought I was dreaming."

"And we might not have gone in if KC hadn't seen the flower you dropped."

KC's mother laughed. "I shook it out of my hair when they were stuffing me into that space suit," she said. "I prayed someone would spot it there."

The president grinned. "Good thinking, Lois!" He picked up his juice glass. "Here's a toast to KC and Marshall. What would the White House do without you two?"

That night, KC and Marshall were watching TV. Lost and Found chased each other around the apartment.

A buzzer sounded. KC's mom walked over to the door and pressed a button.

"Sorry to disturb you, Ms. Corcoran," Donald's voice said from the wall unit. "I have a package for you."

"For me? Okay, send it up."

A few minutes later, she opened the door. Donald grinned and handed her a long white box.

"What is it, Mom?" KC got up and walked over to the door.

"It looks like flowers," her mother said. She removed the lid. Under a layer of tissue paper lay two dozen yellow roses.

"Oh my goodness!" KC's mom said. "Who would send me roses?"

A small envelope was taped to the box. "There's a note, Mom—read it!" KC said.

KC's mother opened the envelope and

pulled out a card. She read it silently, then began to smile.

"No fair," KC said. "Read it out loud!"

Blushing, Lois Corcoran read the card:

Dear Lois,

Please accept my apology for your terrible experience yesterday. May I make it up to you with dinner at the White House tomorrow night? This time I promise to show up!

Fondly,
Zach Thornton

Fondly? thought KC. *The president asked my mom on a date!*

This is the end of
KIDNAPPED
AT THE CAPITAL.

Turn the page to read
THE SKELETON
IN THE SMITHSONIAN.

THE SKELETON
IN THE
SMITHSONIAN

by **Ron Roy**
illustrated by **Timothy Bush**

1

Pizza with the President

"Why do I have to watch a bunch of disgusting bugs eat their supper?" KC asked. She and Marshall were in the O. Orkin Insect Zoo at the National Museum of Natural History.

"Because," Marshall explained, "Spike has stopped eating, and I want to find out why." Spike was Marshall's pet tarantula. Marshall was crazy about anything with more than four legs.

"Okay, okay," KC said. "But we can only stay for a few minutes. We have to be at the White House at five-thirty."

They passed a beehive behind glass,

then an African termite mound. Some little kids were petting a huge cockroach held by a museum scientist. KC unzipped her backpack, pulled out her camera, and snapped a picture.

Marshall headed right for the tarantulas. A woman was dropping food into a glass-sided container. About ten people were watching. Marshall wriggled his way to the front. He saw two tarantulas pounce on the food. The black spiders were the size of Marshall's hands.

"Gross," KC muttered.

"My tarantula isn't eating," Marshall told the woman. "What can I do?"

"What have you been feeding it?" the woman asked.

"Mostly flies," Marshall said. "And crickets, when I can find them."

"It may be bored with that food," the woman said. "Tarantulas like variety." She put her hand on the tarantula tank. "These guys get beetles, grubs, crickets, cockroaches, moths, and other insects." The woman wrote something on a piece of paper and handed it to Marshall. "Try this place in Florida. They sell live insects online," she said. "They'll send them right to your door."

Marshall thanked the woman. "Good luck," she called as he and KC walked toward the exit.

"Well, that was just super," KC said in the elevator. "I may *never* eat again."

Marshall grinned. "Spiders have to live, too," he said. "What would the world be like without them?"

"Much better!" KC said. She gave him

a friendly bump with her shoulder.

Marshall returned the nudge as the elevator door opened. When they reached the exit, a family of tourists was staggering in. "It must be a hundred degrees out there," the woman said, wiping her face with a hankie. The man smiled when he felt the air-conditioning.

"I wanna see the bugs!" their little boy said.

KC and Marshall stepped out into the heat. It was five o'clock, but the sun was still beating down on Washington.

A red-faced man in shorts walked up to the museum's entrance. "Hope you're not planning to go to the Smithsonian Castle," he said to KC and Marshall. He tilted his head toward the red building across the Mall lawn. "The hottest day of the year and the air-conditioning breaks down!"

KC glanced over at the stone building that looked like a castle. A stream of people hurried outside. Two guards stood at the exit, making sure everyone left. Near the entrance was parked a white van with ACE AIR-CONDITIONING on the side.

"They sure don't look happy," KC said as they headed for Pennsylvania Avenue. President Zachary Thornton was waiting for them at the White House. Ever since KC and Marshall had saved him from evil scientists, he'd been their friend.

"Is your mom coming tonight, too?" Marshall asked KC.

She nodded. "The president is sending a car to pick her up at work."

Marshall smiled at KC. "President Thornton really likes her."

KC blushed. "So? They just hang out together," she said.

Marshall rolled his eyes. "KC, you and I hang out together. When adults hang out, it's called dating," he said.

KC was quiet for the rest of the walk to the White House.

They went to the special entrance where a marine guard stood on duty. He smiled when he saw the kids.

"Hi, KC. Hi, Marshall," the marine said. "The president is expecting you."

"Hi, Arnold," KC said. "We're having pizza with him and my mom."

The marine winked. "Yeah, I know. She got here a little while ago. I think the president is sweet on her."

"Told you," Marshall said to KC.

"It's not serious!" KC insisted.

They followed Arnold to the president's private apartment. Arnold rapped on the door and a voice said, "Come in."

The president and KC's mom were seated at a table, drinking lemonade. President Thornton was setting up a Monopoly board. His fluffy cat, George, was purring on his lap. "Hi, KC. Hi, Marshall," he said. "Have some lemonade. You look hot."

"It's roasting out there," Marshall said. "And guess what? The air-conditioning broke in the Smithsonian building."

"The Castle?" the president asked. "They'll get it fixed by tomorrow, I'm sure."

KC gave her mom a kiss. "Where's the pizza?" she asked.

"The cook's making it right now," KC's mom said. She looked across at the president. "What is he putting on it, Zachary?"

KC couldn't get used to hearing her mom call the President of the United States by his first name. KC called him sir or Mr. President.

The president grinned. "Rat tails and toad tongues," he said.

The vice president, Mary Kincaid, walked into the room. She said hello, then handed the president a folded piece of paper. "I hope this is a gag, sir."

President Thornton quickly read what was on the paper. When he looked up, his grin was gone. "Someone is claiming to be the heir to James Smithson," he said.

"Who's James Smithson?" KC asked.

"He was the man who started the Smithsonian Institution," the president said. "He was a wealthy British scientist who died in the 1800s. Mr. Smithson left his money to his nephew, about half a million dollars. Smithson's will stated that if the nephew died without children, the money should come to the United States to create the Smithsonian Institution."

The president scooted George off his lap and walked to a shelf. He pulled out a book and opened it to a picture of James Smithson. "When the nephew died without heirs," President Thornton went on, "Congress received the money and the Smithsonian Castle was begun in 1847. Since then, many other buildings have been added."

"And now someone is claiming to be an heir?" KC's mom asked. "So that half a million dollars . . ."

"That's right." The president glanced down at the note. "This man—Leonard Fisher—claims that the money used to start the Smithsonian Institution really belongs to him. And with interest, it would be worth millions of dollars!"

Everyone stared at the president. "Can he do that?" KC asked.

"He can say whatever he wants," the president said. He turned to the vice president. "Mary, I'd like to meet with Mr. Fisher tonight, if possible."

A man in a white jacket entered the room carrying a pizza. "Put it next to the Monopoly board, please," the president said. Then he picked up the dice. "Since I'm the president," he said, "I get to roll first."

2

The Unknown Heir

KC and Marshall were clearing up the pizza plates when Leonard Fisher and his attorney were announced.

"We appreciate your coming on such short notice," the president told the two men.

"No problem," Mr. A. C. Rook, the attorney, said. He smiled, showing a row of small, sharp teeth.

Leonard Fisher sat down on a couch. He wore a blue jacket over a white shirt with no tie. "Thanks for inviting us," he said. "I want to get this settled so I can get back to work soon."

"Oh, what do you do, Mr. Fisher?" Mary Kincaid asked.

"I'm a landscape designer," he said. "When rich people want a nice garden, they call me."

Just then Mr. Fisher sneezed. Grabbing a paper napkin, he wiped his eyes and nose. "Sorry, I'm allergic to those." He pointed to a blue vase of flowers on the table.

"You're allergic to flowers?" Mary Kincaid asked.

"Just those tall ones, the lilies," Mr. Fisher said.

Mary Kincaid made a phone call. A few seconds later, a maid came and removed the vase.

"Well, why don't we get started?" Rook said. "You've read Mr. Fisher's claim.

Have you any questions, Mr. President?"

"Yes, I do," the president said. "Mr. Fisher claims to be James Smithson's heir. Can you tell us, Mr. Fisher, just how you are related to him?"

Leonard Fisher nodded. "Sure. James Smithson left his money to his nephew, Henry Hungerford. What no one knows is that Hungerford had a child. A son. He was my great-great-grandfather. When Hungerford died, the money came to the United States." Mr. Fisher tapped himself on the chest. "That money should be mine."

"But it's always been thought that Mr. Hungerford died without getting married or having children," Mary Kincaid said. "That's why the money came to the United States."

Mr. Fisher shrugged. "I guess everyone thought wrong," he said. He glanced at his lawyer.

The lawyer pulled a thick document from his briefcase. He placed it on the table. "These papers prove our claim," Rook said, showing his teeth. "A direct line from Henry Hungerford to my client."

"May I ask why you waited until now to come forward?" Mary Kincaid asked as she picked up the stapled pages.

"My client only learned about his connection to Hungerford recently," Rook explained.

Mary Kincaid glanced at the first page, then passed the document to the president. "Our lawyers will need some time to look these over," she said. "Naturally, the documents have to be examined very carefully. We need to be sure Mr. Fisher really is related to James Smithson. We may require more than a few sheets of paper."

"What other proof do you need?" the lawyer asked. "Mr. Fisher is directly related to James Smithson through Smithson's nephew."

"Our attorneys will decide that," said the president. "No one wants to cheat Mr. Fisher out of what is rightfully his."

The adults looked at each other.

"Um, how about DNA?" Marshall asked.

Everyone turned to look at him. Except KC. She was watching Mr. Fisher. He had a funny smile on his face.

Marshall blushed and took a sip of his lemonade.

"Well, I was thinking, why not compare James Smithson's DNA with Mr. Fisher's?" he asked. "If they're related, the DNA will prove it."

Mr. Fisher smiled at Marshall. "That's a good idea," he said, "except for one thing. We don't have any of James Smithson's DNA."

"Yes, we do!" KC said. She pointed through a window. "His body is in the Smithsonian Castle."

"It is?" the lawyer asked.

"Yes," the president said. "Smithson's remains are in a sarcophagus on permanent display there."

"Then that's perfect," the lawyer said, beaming at Leonard Fisher. "My client will be glad to have the tests whenever you want."

President Thornton was quiet for a moment. Then he stood up. "Right. We'll open the crypt to take a DNA sample from James Smithson," he said. "Mary, will you ask my secretary to arrange that for tomorrow?"

Mary Kincaid nodded. "Yes, sir."

Rook snapped his briefcase shut. "My client is staying at the Dupont Inn," he said. "We'll wait to hear from you."

Mary Kincaid stood up. "Thank you, gentlemen," she said, walking them to the door. "Someone will contact Mr. Fisher for his DNA sample."

After Mr. Fisher and his lawyer had gone, the president looked wearily at KC and Marshall. "If Mr. Fisher is Henry Hungerford's heir, the United States may lose the Smithsonian."

"Maybe the DNA won't match," said Marshall.

"You're right, Marshall," the president said, straightening up. "We should keep a positive attitude. Anyway, we'll know one way or the other after we open that sarcophagus tomorrow."

"Can we watch?" KC asked.

The president gave KC and Marshall a sly look. "Have you ever seen a hundred-and-seventy-year-old skeleton?"

3
Spying and Lying

"At least the air-conditioning is working again," KC whispered to Marshall. They were in the Smithsonian Castle with the president and two scientists. It was only nine o'clock in the morning, so the building wasn't open to the public yet.

"Why are you whispering?" Marshall asked with a grin. "Scared of ghosts?"

"You two are about to witness history," the president broke in. "Without that gift from James Smithson, Washington, D.C., would be a different place."

"All set, Mr. President," one of the scientists said. "This should only take a few minutes." She was wearing rubber gloves and carried a specimen jar.

They were in the main room of the Castle. To the left was another, smaller room. Through the open arch, KC could see a gray casket resting on a stone pedestal. The president entered the room first, and the others followed.

The marble sarcophagus stood in the center of the room. There was no other furniture. A small sign told the public that inside the casket were the remains of James Smithson, who died in 1829.

KC felt herself trembling. She hoped Marshall wouldn't notice.

"Okay, let's do it," President Thornton said, moving back to stand next to KC and Marshall. His voice sounded hollow in the quiet room. They watched one scientist insert the flat end of a crowbar into the crack under the sarcophagus lid. Then both scientists leaned on the bar until the lid was raised high enough for them to get their hands beneath it. They carefully removed the lid and set it aside.

The president put his hands on KC's and Marshall's shoulders. "Come meet James Smithson," he said quietly.

The kids stepped forward. KC felt as if she were in a spooky movie. She expected to see a fully preserved body, wrapped like a mummy. But lying on the bottom of the casket were only bones and bits of clothing. Long gray hair still covered part of the skull.

The female scientist reached in while her partner held the open jar. She removed a few hairs from the skull and dropped them into the container. Then she turned and looked at the president. "Anything else, sir?" she asked.

"That's all you need?" he asked. "A few hairs?"

The scientist smiled. "That's all we need."

"When will we know?" the president asked. "I hate to rush you, but we need an answer as soon as possible."

"We have our best people working on this," the scientist said. "In a couple of hours we'll be able to tell how these samples compare with Mr. Fisher's hair."

President Thornton smiled. "Thank you."

The scientists replaced the sarcophagus lid, sealed the specimen jar, and left the building.

The president said good-bye to the kids on the front steps of the Castle. KC and Marshall watched him step into his waiting car. When it pulled away, they began walking home.

"So if Mr. Fisher is telling the truth, he'll be a zillionaire by tomorrow," said Marshall.

KC and Marshall headed toward the Capitol. When they passed a large garden, KC took her camera out of her backpack. She snapped a picture of Marshall in front of some white blossoms covered with monarch butterflies.

KC studied one of the blossoms. "That's funny," she said.

"What's funny?" Marshall asked. He was watching a fat yellow bee.

"The sign says these are lilies," KC told

him. "Remember when Leonard Fisher sneezed yesterday? He said he was allergic to the lilies in the vase. But the flowers in the vase didn't look anything like these."

"So maybe he was allergic to some other flower," Marshall said.

"I think gardeners should know one flower from another," KC said as they walked.

She gave Marshall a sideways look. "Another thing," KC added. "Did you notice the look on Mr. Fisher's face when you mentioned DNA?"

"No," Marshall said.

"Well, I was watching him," KC said. "When you brought up DNA, he got all smiley."

Marshall laughed. "Wouldn't you be

happy if you found out you could inherit a lot of money?"

KC shook her head. "It wasn't that kind of smile, Marsh. It was sneaky, like the way you smile when you're cheating at Monopoly."

"I don't cheat!" Marshall said.

KC grinned. "Yeah, and that hundred-dollar bill just happened to stick to your elbow last night."

A few minutes later, they were waiting for a light across the street from the Dupont Inn. "Isn't that where Mr. Fisher said he was staying?" KC asked.

"I think so," Marshall said. "Why?"

KC pushed the button for the WALK sign so they could cross. "We should spy on him."

"KC, the president can take care of this

Smithsonian stuff," Marshall said. "He doesn't need you."

KC took Marshall by the arm. "Let's at least see if Fisher is there."

The kids passed through a revolving door into the hotel.

The lobby was decorated to look like a tropical island. There were palm trees in big pots, and pictures of sandy beaches hanging on the walls. Soft music came from hidden speakers.

KC walked up to the desk. A tall man stood behind it typing on a computer. "Excuse me," KC said. "My friend is feeling faint from the heat. Could he have something to drink?"

"No problem." The man pointed to a small table. "There are drinks and pastries over there. Help yourself."

"Thank you," KC said. She turned away, then spun back. "By the way, is Mr. Fisher in?"

"Mr. Leonard Fisher, the musician?" the clerk asked. "Yes, he went up about ten minutes ago."

KC stared at him. "Musician? I thought he was a gardener," she said. "Are there *two* Leonard Fishers staying here?"

"I don't think so." The man tapped a few keys on his computer. "No, it's showing only one Leonard Fisher. I was here when he checked in. He was carrying a long black case. When I asked about it, he said he played in a band. Would you like me to ring Mr. Fisher in his room?"

"Oh, no, thank you," KC said. "We'll just wait. We want to surprise him."

"Suit yourself," the clerk said.

KC sighed and sat in an armchair where she could watch the elevators. "Gardener, musician. Marsh, there's something very weird going on," she said.

Marshall bit into a jelly doughnut and relaxed in the air-conditioned lobby. "I know someone who has an overactive imagination," he said. He wiggled deeper into his chair. "I wonder how much a room costs in this place."

"A lot more than you have," KC said. "Unless you use some of that Monopoly money you stole."

"I didn't steal any—"

"Shhh! There he is!" KC said. She ducked behind a tree as Leonard Fisher stepped out of the elevator. He was wearing shorts, sneakers, and a light blue shirt. He was also carrying a black instrument case. The case was as tall as KC and had a handle on the side.

KC and Marshall watched Leonard Fisher cross the lobby and walk outside.

KC counted to five, then stood up. "Come on, Marshall," she whispered. "Don't let him see you!"

KC and Marshall followed Leonard Fisher. When he stopped to buy a newspaper, they hid behind a Dumpster. When he looked in a window at some clothing, they slipped into an alley.

"I feel like a jerk," Marshall said. "Tell me again why we're following this guy?"

"Because I don't trust him," KC said.

Marshall snorted. "You don't trust him? You don't *know* him, KC."

Before KC could respond, Fisher continued walking.

KC and Marshall followed.

"Can you read what it says on the back of his shirt?" KC asked.

Marshall squinted. "Um, I think it says CENTIPEDE something."

KC squinted, too. "No, I think it says CELLOPHANE something."

"Maybe it says CELLO PLAYER," Marshall tried.

Just then Fisher stopped again. He set the black case on the ground and bent down and tied his sneaker lace.

KC whipped out her camera and snapped a picture. She heard a whirring sound and realized that she had just used the last frame. She popped out the roll and put it in her pocket.

When KC looked up again, Leonard Fisher had disappeared.

"Where did he go?" she asked, turning to look all around her. There were plenty of people carrying briefcases, shopping bags, and pocketbooks. But KC saw no one with a musician's case.

"Maybe he went down there," Marshall said. A few yards away, a ramp sloped down to an underground parking garage.

"Let's look," KC said, already walking down the ramp.

The underground garage was quiet and dark. Hundreds of cars, vans, and small trucks were parked in lines. KC smelled gasoline, dust, and dampness.

"Do you see him?" she whispered, peering into the dim corners.

"Um, can we go?" Marshall asked. "This place is creeping me out."

"Yeah, okay," KC said. They walked

back up the ramp into daylight. KC realized that she had goose bumps on her arms.

"I want to drop my film off and buy another roll," she told Marshall. "And when we get home, we're going to play Monopoly again. And this time, don't cheat!"

"I don't have to cheat," Marshall said, tapping the side of his head. "I'm a better player than you."

KC chased him all the way to their building.

4
The Cemetery Bus

The next morning, KC and Marshall took a few shortcuts and reached the camera shop in ten minutes.

KC paid, then opened the cardboard packet that held the pictures and negatives. Marshall looked over her shoulder. There were pictures of KC's kittens, one of Marshall in the garden, and one of the kids petting a cockroach in the Museum of Natural History.

"Here he is," KC said. In the snapshot, Leonard Fisher was bending over to tie his sneaker lace. Next to him rested the black instrument case.

"Before we lost him," Marshall said.

The picture showed the back of Fisher's shirt, but the words printed there weren't clear enough to read. "CELERY something something," KC muttered.

"Wait a sec, I have an idea," Marshall said.

He turned to the clerk. "Can you make this picture bigger?"

"Sure, but it would cost six dollars and take about a week," the clerk said. "I'd have to send it out."

She reached under the counter and pulled out a magnifying glass. "Here, try this," she suggested.

"Thanks a lot!" KC said. She placed the round magnifying glass over the picture of Leonard Fisher. The words on his shirt were suddenly clear.

"CEMETERY STAFF, BOWIE, MARYLAND," Marshall read out loud. He and KC stared at each other.

"Cemetery staff?" KC said. "He told us he made gardens for rich people!"

KC slid the pictures back into the packet. She tucked it into her backpack and headed for the door.

Marshall thanked the clerk and followed KC. "Why would the guy lie about his job?" he asked.

"I don't know," KC said, "but it can't be good."

"What would your mom say if she heard you say that?" Marshall asked.

KC started humming over Marshall's voice.

"She'd say, 'Katherine Christine, don't jump to conclusions!'" Marshall trilled.

He sounded a lot like KC's mom.

KC stopped and looked at Marshall. "Marsh, don't you think it's weird that Leonard Fisher told the president he was a gardener but told the hotel guy he was a musician?" she asked. "And what's up with that shirt?"

"Just because his shirt has CEME-TERY written on it doesn't mean he's lying," Marshall said. "I have a shirt with a picture of a beetle on the back, but I'm not an insect."

"Says who?" KC asked, walking faster.

"Very funny," Marshall said. "And where are we going?"

"Back to the Dupont Inn."

"Oh, brother," Marshall muttered under his breath.

"Don't worry," KC said. "All I want to

do is ask him whether he's a gardener, a musician, or a gravedigger."

Marshall hooted.

"And don't tell me he has three jobs," KC said.

When they walked into the lobby, the same clerk was behind the counter. "Back for another breakfast?" he asked, raising an eyebrow.

"No, thank you," KC said. She gave him her brightest smile. "We need to talk to Leonard Fisher."

The man shook his head. "I'm afraid that's not possible. Mr. Fisher is gone for the day."

"Where did he go?" KC asked.

The clerk sighed. "Miss, I can't give out that kind of information," he said. "Now if you'll excuse me, I—"

"Probably gone home to Bowie, Maryland, right?" Marshall asked.

"That would be my guess," the man said. His phone rang and he picked it up. He turned his back on KC and Marshall.

They walked back out through the revolving doors. "Pretty clever, Marsh," KC said.

"No problem," Marshall said.

KC unzipped her pack and counted her money. "I think I have enough," she said.

"For what?" Marshall asked.

"Two bus fares."

"Uh-oh," Marshall muttered. "I have a feeling I know where we're going."

KC led Marshall toward a bus stop. "If your feeling is Bowie, Maryland, you're right," she said.

"But that's . . . that's three towns away!" said Marshall.

A man in a white shirt and necktie was sitting on the bench reading a newspaper. The headline said HEAT WAVE STRANGLES D.C.

"Excuse me, do you know which bus goes to Bowie, Maryland?" KC asked him.

"I think you want the number thirteen," he said, pulling a bus schedule out of his pocket. He studied the schedule for a moment, then folded it back up. "Yes, thirteen is the one. It should be here in a few minutes."

"So how do we find Leonard Fisher when we get there?" Marshall asked KC.

KC hadn't thought that far ahead, but she was saved from having to answer Marshall. A silver bus with a 13 in the

front window rolled to a stop. They climbed aboard the nearly empty bus. KC paid the driver, and she and Marshall took the seat right behind him.

"At least it's air-conditioned," Marshall said as the bus pulled back into the traffic and headed east.

KC inched up to talk to the driver. "Excuse me, is Bowie a big town?"

The bus driver shook his head. "It's a pretty small place," he said, turning down his radio. "What takes you there?"

"We're looking for someone," KC said. "He's a . . . a friend. We want to surprise him, but we don't know where he works. He's either a gardener or a musician."

Marshall sank lower into his seat. "Or a gravedigger," he murmured just loudly enough for KC to hear.

"Oh yeah," KC told the driver. "He might work at a cemetery."

"Well, there's only one cemetery in Bowie," the driver said. "We pass it just before we get downtown." He looked up into his mirror. "So do you want to go into town, or should I drop you off at the cemetery?"

KC swallowed. "At the cemetery, please."

5
Caught in the Act

KC sat back and hummed along with the music coming from the radio. She knew Marshall was looking at her, so she hummed louder.

"Why do I hang out with you?" Marshall asked.

KC knew he didn't expect an answer, so she didn't give him one.

"Wow!" The bus driver leaned forward and turned up the radio. "Did you hear that?" he said.

The music had stopped, and a reporter with a very smooth voice was speaking: *"According to White House officials, it* has been determined that Leonard Fisher is a direct relative of James Smithson. Smithson is the man whose money started the Smithsonian Institution over one hundred and fifty years ago. Today, Fisher's DNA was compared with Smithson's. It was a definite match. Fisher's claim that the Smithsonian fortune is his seems to be true."

KC leaned forward as far as she could. Then she heard a different voice.

"As Mr. Leonard Fisher's attorney, I can state that he is very happy that his claim is being honored. But he has no intention of taking over the Smithsonian. He will settle for one hundred million dollars, only a fraction of the total worth of all the Smithsonian buildings and their contents."

The reporter took over again. "*White House officials will comment later today. Stay tuned for more on this modern rags-to-riches story of a common man who became a multimillionaire!*"

"Imagine, a hundred million smackers!" said the driver.

"Well, that's it," Marshall said to KC. "Leonard Fisher really is related to James Smithson."

"But then why was he lying about his job?" KC insisted.

Marshall sighed. "KC, we don't know if he was," he said. "It's possible that he *is* a gardener and a musician and he works for a cemetery."

KC wasn't satisfied with that answer. She looked out the window and let her mind wander back to when she'd first met

Fisher, in the White House. Something about him still bothered her.

The bus driver's voice broke into KC's thoughts. "The cemetery's just ahead on the left," he said. Glancing into his rearview mirror, he added, "You sure you want me to leave you here?"

"Yes!" KC said.

"What time will the bus come by again?" Marshall asked.

"I go back to D.C. in ten minutes," the driver said. "But I make the same trip again in about an hour. If you're waiting here, I'll pick you up."

"We'll be here!" Marshall told him.

The driver flashed his left-turn signal and pulled over. "Have a nice time," he joked as the door swooshed open. "And good luck finding your friend."

"Thanks a lot," KC said. She and Marshall got off the bus. The driver waved and pulled back onto the road. In a minute the bus had disappeared around a corner.

The kids were standing in the grass on the side of a road. There were no buildings nearby. The road into the cemetery passed through a gate attached to two stone pillars. One of the pillars held a sign that said:

BOWIE CEMETERY
VISITING HOURS:
DAWN TO DUSK

"Come on," KC said. "Let's see if Leonard Fisher is in there."

They walked through the open gate. Birds were calling to each other in the pine trees. Fresh flowers had been placed

near several of the graves. The grass was neatly cut and the bushes seemed well taken care of.

Marshall looked at his watch. "We have to be back at the gate in fifty-six minutes."

KC laughed. "Don't worry, we will," she said.

A blue car was parked at the edge of the road. KC watched a woman take a box of flowers and some gardening tools out of the trunk. A small white dog ran around on the grass, looking as if it wanted to play.

The woman noticed the kids and waved. "Beautiful day!" she chirped.

"Is your dog friendly?" Marshall asked.

"Too friendly sometimes! Happy, come to Mommy," the woman called.

The dog went scampering over. His

owner scooped him off the ground, walked over to Marshall, and thrust the dog into his arms. "His name is Happy." Happy licked Marshall's face and wriggled with joy.

"Do you know someone named Leonard Fisher?" KC asked the woman.

The woman thought for a moment. "Hmmm, Fisher, Fisher," she said. "I don't think so. When did Mr. Fisher pass away?"

Marshall snorted.

KC gave him a poke with her elbow. "He's still alive," she said. "I think he may work here."

The woman smiled. "Then I definitely don't know him. I'm from out of town, just doing some planting on Aunt Lucy's grave."

"Thanks anyway," KC said.

Marshall set Happy on the ground, and he and KC continued to follow the road as it curved into the cemetery.

Behind them KC heard the woman say, "No, Happy, stay here with Mommy. You can't play with those children!"

Marshall grinned slyly. "'Mommy'?" he whispered. He and KC cracked up.

Just then they saw a white van driving slowly down the road. It stopped about thirty feet from where KC and Marshall were standing.

A man in jeans, a baseball cap, and sunglasses climbed out of the van. Around his waist he wore a wide leather tool belt. He reached into the van, pulled out some hedge clippers, and tucked them into one of the loops on his belt. Then he removed his hat and glasses and wiped his face on his sleeve. On the back of his shirt were the words CEMETERY STAFF, BOWIE, MARYLAND.

When he turned around, KC gasped. The man was Leonard Fisher!

6
Creepy Crypt

Leonard Fisher walked to the rear of his van, opened the door, and dragged out a lawn mower. KC heard him grunt as he lowered the machine to the ground.

Fisher reached back in and pulled out a red gas can. He unscrewed the cap from the mower's gas tank and poured in the gas. After recapping the tank, he yanked a few times on the mower's starter cord. The engine sputtered, then roared to life.

"He's a lawn guy!" Marshall whispered from their hiding spot. When they'd realized who the man was, they'd scooted behind some trees.

"Told you he lied," KC mumbled.

They watched Fisher mow the grass around a few shrubs and tombstones. He kept looking over his shoulder, as if he suspected someone was watching him.

KC and Marshall lay flat on the fallen pine needles under a large tree to make themselves less noticeable.

Leonard Fisher brought the mower back to his van, then let the engine die. He yanked the hedge clippers from his belt and walked over to some bushes next to a small stone building. He started to prune the bushes, stopping every few snips to look over his shoulder. Then he stopped cutting and stuck the clippers back into his belt. He walked quickly over to the van and opened the side door.

What he took out this time made KC

grab Marshall's arm. It was the black instrument case! Fisher held the case by the handle on its side, then nudged the van door shut with his shoulder.

As still as statues, KC and Marshall watched Fisher carry the case away from the van. He returned to the small building. To KC, it looked like a stone cottage from a fairy tale. Leonard Fisher set the case down and pulled a key ring from his pocket.

"What's he doing? Can you see?" KC whispered. A bush partly blocked her view.

Marshall stretched out until he could see better. "He's unlocking that little house," he said. "He's going inside!"

KC got up on her knees. "Come on!" she whispered.

Crouching, the kids scooted over and hid next to the white van. When KC looked through the window, she saw a square plastic sign on the front seat.

She poked Marshall and pointed at the sign: ACE AIR-CONDITIONING. "This van was in front of the Smithsonian Castle the other day!" she whispered.

KC and Marshall tiptoed on the freshly cut grass to the side of the little building. The walls were smooth gray stone, and the sloping roof was slate.

KC peeked around the building's corner. The structure had been built partly underground. The door was open wide, and two stone steps led down to the inside.

A small brass plate was fastened to the outside. In faded letters it said HERE

LIE HOMER AND ESTHER FISHER,
IN ETERNAL REST.

KC gulped. This was a crypt, where
cemeteries put people's coffins instead of
burying them. She looked at Marshall to
see if he'd figured it out.

His eyes were huge and his face had
turned gray.

Holding her breath, KC moved to the
front of the crypt. Marshall had his hand
on her back. His hand was trembling.

There was no light in the stone building, but KC could see Leonard Fisher
kneeling with his back to the door. There
were two stone coffins in the crypt, one on
each side of where Fisher knelt. One of
the coffins was closed. The other was not.
Its lid was off and leaning against the wall.

On the floor next to Fisher's knees was

the instrument case. It was open. Fisher had tossed his tool belt and the clippers into the top half.

But it was the bottom half of the case that grabbed KC's attention. In it, on blue velvet lining, lay a small skeleton.

Suddenly KC felt Marshall stumble into her. She put out her hands to stop herself from falling.

Leonard Fisher wheeled around. When he saw the kids, his mouth opened in surprise. KC watched him trying to figure out where he'd seen them before.

Then he grinned. "Well, hello," he said. "What are *you* doing here?" As he spoke, his right hand slowly moved to the instrument case. With one quick motion, he flipped it shut.

"We followed you!" KC said.

Fisher was still grinning, but his eyes looked nervous.

"You followed me? Why?"

"Because you lied to the president!" Marshall said.

Fisher shook his head. "I lied? About what?"

Before KC could answer him, Fisher jumped forward as fast as a rattlesnake strikes. He grabbed her and Marshall by the wrists and pulled them into the crypt. "Let's keep this private, shall we?" he said, releasing their hands. "Besides, it's cooler in here."

He leaned against the wall by the door. It was still open, letting sunlight into the damp chamber.

Fisher took a pack of gum from one of his pockets and held it out to the kids.

Neither took any. Fisher shrugged, slid out a piece, and began unwrapping it. "Now, you were saying . . . ?"

"You told the president you were some fancy gardener, but you really work in a cemetery," KC said.

She pointed to the instrument case. "And there's a skeleton in there. I saw it!"

Suddenly Marshall understood. "You switched skeletons!" he cried. "You're not related to James Smithson! You knew they'd check his DNA, so you put one of your dead relatives in the sarcophagus!" Marshall pointed to the open coffin. "It was him, wasn't it?"

"You're pretty smart kids," Fisher said. "Yeah, I switched. The one I left in the museum is my great-great-grandfather." He nodded toward the instrument case.

"And that's James Smithson. But by the time anyone figures that out, I'll be long gone—with a hundred million bucks in my pocket. I'll disappear forever."

"No, you won't!" KC said. "We're telling the president as soon as we get back!"

Fisher laughed. "Back? You're not going back," he said. "At least not till I'm far away from here."

He ran up the steps and out of the crypt. Before KC or Marshall could react, he'd slammed the door.

7
Trapped!

"Stop!" Marshall yelled. He leaped toward the door but tripped on KC's feet. They both fell over, then scrambled up and tried to force the metal door open. It stayed solidly shut.

"He locked it," Marshall said. "What are we gonna do?"

It was totally dark. KC couldn't even see Marshall, though she knew he was standing right next to her. "I'm sitting down," she said, "so we don't trip over each other again."

She hunched down, and she felt Marshall sit next to her. The floor of the crypt was cold, damp stone. KC felt goose bumps racing up her arms.

"Someone will come looking for us," she said. She tried to sound calm.

"Like who?" Marshall said, sounding not at all calm. "No one knows where we are!"

KC realized Marshall was right. They'd taken the number 13 bus without going home, so KC hadn't left a note for her mother. And the president had no idea where they were.

KC started to say that as soon as their parents got worried, they'd come looking. But of course, they wouldn't know where to look. Not even the FBI would find KC and Marshall in a Maryland cemetery.

Then KC remembered the one person who did know where they were.

"The bus driver!" she said. "He said he'd look for us at the gate in an hour. How much time is left, Marsh?"

The hands on Marshall's watch glowed in the dark. "He dropped us off thirty-two minutes ago," he said.

"Okay, so when we don't show up in a half hour, the bus driver will tell somebody we're in the cemetery."

"But, KC, he doesn't know that we're locked in this dumb crypt," Marshall said. "Even if someone comes to the cemetery, they won't know where to look for us!"

"Oh," KC said. She thought for a minute. "There might be more people visiting graves," she said. "We have to make a lot of loud noise. Did you see anything we can bang with?"

"Like what, a drum?" Marshall wisecracked. "KC, this is where they keep dead people. There's nothing in here but two coffins that weigh about a million pounds each."

"And the musician's case," KC said. "Could we use that?"

"I'm not touching that thing," Marshall said. "Did you forget it's filled with bones?"

"Not just bones," KC said. "I saw the hedge clippers in there, too!"

She scrambled over Marshall's knees and crawled around until she felt the instrument case. Her fingers unhooked the clasps, and she lifted the lid. She took a deep breath and reached in, knowing the skeleton was lying there. But her fingers felt the rubber handles of the hedge clippers. They'd fallen on top of the bones when Fisher slammed the case shut.

KC grabbed the heavy clippers and crawled back to Marshall.

"Did you get 'em?" he asked.

"Yes!" KC began banging on the crypt door with the metal blades. The clanging noise bounced around the space.

"I hope it sounds that loud outside," Marshall said.

KC smacked the tool against the door until her arms grew tired, and then Marshall took over.

When Marshall stopped, KC heard a high-pitched noise outside. "Do you hear that?" she asked.

"It's Happy!" Marshall cried. "He's barking! He knows we're in here!"

Marshall dropped the hedge clippers and began yelling. KC and Marshall could

hear the little dog's excited yelping. He sounded close.

"Good dog, Happy!" Marshall yelled. "Happy, go get Mommy! Find Mommy!"

Happy stopped barking. KC and Marshall pressed their ears against the door. Then they heard a wonderful sound. "Is someone in there?" Happy's owner asked.

"Yes!" Marshall screamed.

"Can you get us out?" KC cried.

"There's a big padlock," the woman said. "I can't imagine how I'll get it unlocked."

Happy began to bark again.

"I know!" the woman yelled through the door. "I passed a gas station when I drove here. I'll go there and get someone to break this lock. Will you be all right?"

"We'll be okay," KC said. "But please hurry!"

After she left, the kids slumped back onto the stone floor. The floor was cold, and KC shivered.

"It's f-freezing in this place," Marshall said, shivering. "I'll never complain about the heat again!"

The kids sat, leaning against each other for warmth. KC felt herself growing sleepy. Her eyes closed, but she blinked them open again. Her head felt so heavy. She let her chin fall and closed her eyes. This time she didn't try to open them again.

The next thing she knew, Marshall was shaking her by the shoulder. "KC, wake up! They're here!" he cried.

8
Found

When KC sat up, she felt groggy. She heard a man's voice through the door. "Are you kids all right?" the voice called.

"We're okay!" Marshall yelled back.

"Great, we'll have you out in a jiffy," the voice said. "Stand back while I bust this lock!"

KC and Marshall moved a few feet away from the door. Suddenly they heard a loud smashing sound of metal against metal. The door opened, and sunlight flooded the crypt. Blinking in the sudden light, KC and Marshall staggered up the steps.

The first thing KC saw was Happy, the little white dog. He was straining at his leash, barking and practically dancing with excitement.

Happy's owner was standing with two police officers. A police car was parked a few yards away.

"Thank goodness you're all right!" Happy's owner said.

KC smiled at the woman. "Thank you so much! We would have been trapped in that crypt forever if your dog hadn't found us!"

Marshall got on his knees and gave Happy a big hug. Happy licked Marshall's face and wiggled all over.

"Who locked you kids in there?" the male officer asked. He was a tall man with a friendly face.

"Leonard Fisher," KC said. "We have to hurry! He's getting away!"

"Leonard Fisher?" the officer repeated. "Isn't he the heir to the Smithsonian fortune?"

"Yeah," said Marshall, still holding Happy. "But he's not really an heir!"

KC quickly explained how Leonard Fisher had lied about being related to James Smithson.

"He put his great-great-grandfather's skeleton in the Smithsonian," Marshall added. "Then he stole James Smithson's skeleton and brought it here!" Marshall pointed through the door at the instrument case.

All three adults stared down into the crypt. The bones were easy to see in the sunlight.

"This is a crime scene," the female officer said. She walked to the cruiser and came back with a roll of wide yellow plastic tape. She and her partner quickly wrapped the tape around the crypt.

"Okay, let's go," the male officer said. "Where do you kids live?"

"We're not going home yet," KC told the man.

He looked at her. "So where do you want us to take you?"

"To the White House!" KC said.

Less than an hour later, the kids were sitting across from President Thornton, Vice President Kincaid, and KC's mom. The adults listened wide-eyed as KC told the story.

The kind police officers had called the

White House from their car. They'd been put right through to the vice president. She'd told the president, he'd called KC's mom, and all three had been waiting when the police car arrived.

Now they were in the president's private rooms. A maid had brought in sandwiches and they were all eating lunch. George the cat lay snoozing in a patch of sunshine.

"You went to Maryland on a bus without telling me?" KC's mom said. "If I weren't so relieved, I'd ground you right now!"

"I'm sorry, Mom," KC said. "But we had to follow Leonard Fisher. I just knew there was something weird about him."

"Well, as it turns out, you were right on the money," President Thornton said. He tapped a memo he was holding. "Our FBI agents picked up Mr. Fisher. He admitted everything."

"His idea was very clever," the vice president said. "Fisher assumed that we'd end up comparing his DNA with that of James Smithson. So he simply switched skeletons ahead of time. He never even told his lawyer what he'd done."

"He broke the air-conditioning in the Smithsonian," Marshall said. "Then he pretended to be a repairman so he could go in and swap the skeletons."

The president smiled at Marshall. "When you brought up DNA, Fisher was actually relieved," he said. "He couldn't suggest DNA himself or it would seem suspicious. So he was happy when you did it for him."

"What made you suspect him to begin with?" KC's mom asked.

KC pointed to the vase of tall flowers on the table. "When he came here, he was sneezing and told us he was allergic to lilies," she said. "But there weren't any lilies in the vase!"

"So Fisher wasn't a landscape designer for the rich?" the president said. "I wonder why he lied about that."

"I don't think he wanted you to know he worked for the cemetery," KC said. "He was afraid you'd find out his relatives were buried there and you might figure out his plan."

Mary Kincaid nodded. "I think you're right," she said. "Let's just all be grateful to that little dog."

The president glanced at KC and

Marshall. "I don't know why we need a police force or FBI agents," he said. "With you two on the job, crooks don't stand a chance!"

KC and Marshall blushed.

"Well, I have to get busy," the vice president said. "We have to return the two skeletons to their rightful resting places."

"And I have to get back to my office," KC's mom said, glancing at the president.

President Thornton stood up. "Yes, let me get a car for you, Lois," he said. "I'll call from the other room."

The president and KC's mom left the room together. KC and Marshall were alone with George the cat.

"Gee, that's funny," Marshall said as he reached for a cookie.

"What is?" KC asked.

Marshall grinned at KC. "I wonder why the president had to leave the room to use the phone? There's one right there on that table."

KC couldn't think of a good reason.

"I think they wanted to be alone," Marshall whispered.

"And I think *you* have an overactive imagination!" KC shot back.

"Me? That's the best joke I've heard in a year!"

Just then the door opened. The president and KC's mom walked back in.

"Are you two finished with lunch?" KC's mom asked the kids. "The car is ready for us."

As KC and Marshall got ready to leave, KC stole a glance at her mom and the president. They were standing next to each other by the door. The president's left arm and her mom's right arm were an inch apart.

But their pinkie fingers were touching.

The next day, KC and Marshall stood with the president in the Smithsonian Castle. The same two scientists as before removed the lids from the sarcophagus and a special container holding Smithson's remains. The scientists silently exchanged the two skeletons and replaced the lids. They left the building carrying old Mr. Fisher's skeleton in the container. They told the president they were on their way to Bowie, Maryland.

When the kids followed the president out of the Castle, KC was surprised to find her mom waiting on the steps.

"Mom, what're you doing here?" KC asked.

"I decided to take the day off," her mom said, glancing at the president.

"And I'm taking us all to lunch," the president said. "Your mother and I have something to tell you, KC."

Marshall snorted and gave KC a playful shove. He waggled his eyebrows.

KC returned the shove. She smiled at her mother and the president. "Good," she said. "I love surprises!"

This is the end of
THE SKELETON
IN THE SMITHSONIAN.

Turn the page to read
A SPY IN THE
WHITE HOUSE.

A SPY IN THE WHITE HOUSE

by **Ron Roy**
illustrated by **Timothy Bush**

1
Who's Listening?

"Come on down, George Washington. It's time to go outside," KC said.

The president's cat, George, was sitting on top of the refrigerator.

"Will you get him down, Marshall?" KC asked. "We have to practice for the wedding."

KC Corcoran and Marshall Li were best friends. They lived in Washington, D.C. But today, they were in the White House. KC's mom was going to marry the President of the United States next week!

KC would hold her mom's flowers during the ceremony, and Marshall would be the ring bearer—with George's help.

"What's to practice?" Marshall grumbled. "Your mom says 'I do,' then the president says 'I do,' then it's over."

KC rolled her eyes. "This is a White House wedding, Marsh," she said. "Everything has to be perfect. The whole world will be watching on TV!"

Marshall raised his eyebrows. "I'll be on TV?" he asked.

KC nodded. "We'll all be on TV," she said. "Even George. That's why we have to practice making him walk down the aisle."

Marshall grabbed George while KC opened the door that led out of the president's private quarters.

Arnold, the marine guard on duty, saluted them. "Afternoon, KC," he said. "Afternoon, Marshall."

"Hi, Arnold," the kids said.

Arnold took off one white glove and stroked George under the chin. Then he sneezed.

"Are you allergic to cats?" Marshall asked.

Arnold sniffed. "No, I have a cold and a sore throat," he said with a hoarse voice. KC noticed that Arnold's nose was red. His eyes looked watery and puffy.

"I hope you feel better for the wedding," KC said.

"Thanks," Arnold said. "I'll try."

KC and Marshall left Arnold and walked to the rose garden. Marshall set George down, and KC tied a green ribbon to his collar.

"Why does George need a silly green ribbon?" Marshall asked. "What's wrong with a piece of rope or something?"

"The ribbon matches Mom's dress, my dress, and your vest," KC reminded him. "The wedding is color-coordinated!"

"Maybe I'll get sick like Arnold," Marshall muttered. He looked at his hand. "You know, my skin does look a little green."

"Perfect, you'll fit right into the color scheme!" KC crowed. "Let's get started."

KC pulled a wad of string from her pocket and made a long, straight line on the lawn. "This is where we have to walk," she said to Marshall. "The wedding guests will be sitting in chairs on both sides."

"*I* know that," said Marshall. "But someone had better explain it to George."

George was half under a bush, investigating a line of ants.

"Get him out of there before his ribbon gets tangled," KC said.

Marshall tugged George out from under the bush and set him down near the string.

"Okay!" KC began humming the wedding march. She took small steps over to where the president would be waiting.

"Now it's time for the rings," KC called to Marshall.

"Come on, George, let's walk," said Marshall as he bent to pick up the cat's ribbon. But George had a different idea. He bolted across the lawn, the ribbon flying behind him.

"Hey, that's the wrong way!" Marshall yelled. He and KC chased after George, who disappeared in some shrubbery.

"Marsh, why'd you let him run away?"

KC asked. She peeked into a thorny bush covered with pink rose blossoms.

"I didn't *let* him do anything!" Marshall said. "I'm not an animal trainer, you know."

"I hope he doesn't take off during the wedding," KC said. "He'll have the wedding rings around his neck."

"That's why we're practicing," Marshall said. "And so far it's a big flop!"

The kids searched under all the rose-bushes. No George.

They crawled on their hands and knees and peeked under the hedges. George stayed out of sight.

They looked up in the tall trees that lined the fences surrounding the White House. They saw birds and squirrels, but no large, fluffy cat with a green ribbon tied to his collar.

Twenty minutes later, they still hadn't found George. They had searched most of the grounds around the White House.

"Should we check outside the fence?" Marshall asked. "Maybe he snuck under."

"I know!" KC said. She dug a bag of Kitty Kandy out of her pocket and started shaking it.

Traffic whizzed by on Pennsylvania Avenue. Horns honked, brakes squealed, and a motorcycle roared past.

"George will never hear you rattling that stuff," Marshall said.

Just then George walked out of the hedges. KC gave Marshall a look.

Marshall ignored her and picked up George. "Bad cat!" he said. "You could get smushed out there!"

KC gave George a treat and put the

bag back in her pocket. "That's weird. George smells like mint. I think he's been in the herb garden," she told Marshall.

Marshall rolled his eyes. "You're just imagining another mystery," he teased.

KC checked her watch. "Well, there's one thing I'm not imagining. We've got to go! The press conference is starting!"

"Can't we skip it?" Marshall asked. "Let's go to Rock Creek Park and look for bugs!"

"We can go to the park anytime," KC said. "But how often does my mom marry the president?"

"You really want to see all those reporters," Marshall said.

"I can't help it," KC said. "Someday when I'm a big Washington reporter, maybe I'll interview you!"

She and Marshall hurried to the Oval Office. When they burst through the door, they saw about twenty reporters waving their hands and aiming microphones toward the president.

KC's mom and the president were sitting side by side on a long white sofa. Lois smiled at KC and patted the seat next to hers.

KC sat down by her mom. George jumped out of Marshall's arms and hopped onto President Thornton's lap.

KC felt embarrassed when everyone stared at her. Her mother took her hand and squeezed it.

Marshall watched from the back of the room. For the next fifteen minutes, the president and Lois answered a lot of questions. Everyone wanted to know how they met. Everyone wanted to know about the wedding and who would be invited.

Then one female reporter asked the president where he and Lois were going on their honeymoon.

"We're keeping that information in the family," the president said, smiling as the cameras clicked away.

"Ms. Corcoran, can you tell us about your wedding dress?" the woman asked. "What does it look like? Who designed it for you?"

KC had seen her mother's pale green dress. It was hanging in a closet upstairs in the White House. KC thought it was the most gorgeous dress in the world. She couldn't wait to see her mother wear it on her wedding day.

"That's going to be a surprise for the

wedding," Lois said. "But I can tell you this much—it's beautiful!"

The president set George on the floor and stood up. "I'm afraid that has to be the last question," he said. "Lois and I have a lot of plans to make. Thank you all for coming!"

The reporters gathered their stuff and filed out of the room.

"Well, that wasn't so bad, was it?" the president asked when all the press had gone.

"Why didn't you say where you're going on your honeymoon?" Marshall asked.

"We don't want a thousand reporters and helicopters buzzing around," the president said. He took Lois by the hand. "Now let's go find out what's for lunch."

The next morning, KC, her mom, and

Marshall arrived at the White House to have breakfast with the president. They found him in his dining room, staring at the newspaper.

"You're not going to believe this," the president said. He turned the paper so they could all see.

Covering almost the whole front page was a picture of the Island Paradise Hotel in Maui, Hawaii. Beneath the picture were these words:

PRESIDENT AND BRIDE TO
HONEYMOON IN HAWAIIAN
ISLAND HOTEL

2

There's a Spy in
the White House

"How did they find out?" KC asked.

"I wish I knew," the president said grimly. "They even found the hotel on Maui."

He glanced at Lois, KC, and Marshall. "I don't suppose any of you accidentally let the cat out of the bag?"

"I certainly didn't," Lois said. "I want our honeymoon to be private."

"I didn't either," said KC.

They all looked at Marshall.

"I know how to keep a secret!" cried Marshall. "Besides, I didn't know the name of the hotel."

"Well, someone found out, and they told Darla Darling," Lois said.

Darla Darling wrote the society column for the *Star* newspaper. Her picture was at the top of her column.

"I saw her at the press conference yesterday," Marshall told them.

"Yes, she was the reporter who asked about the honeymoon and my dress," Lois said.

"Maybe someone at the hotel blabbed to her," Marshall suggested.

The president shook his head. "The hotel people in Hawaii didn't know our real names," he said. "Lois and I were registered as Mr. and Mrs. Smith."

"Well, I'm going to get to the bottom of this," Lois said. She picked up a telephone and called the newspaper. She asked to speak to Darla Darling. A few seconds later, she hung up.

"Her voice mail," Lois explained. " 'Ms. Darling is on assignment and not available.' "

The president picked up a different telephone and asked Vice President Mary Kincaid to come in. When she arrived, the president showed her the newspaper.

"How did Darla Darling find out?" the vice president asked. "That was top-secret information!"

"None of us leaked it," the president said. "Could it have been someone on my staff?"

"I can't imagine that," Mary said. "They knew you and Lois wanted your honeymoon spot kept a secret."

"Secret or not, Darla Darling found

out," Lois said. "And she didn't hear it from some little bird!"

"No, but it could have been a little bug," Marshall said.

Everyone looked at him.

"What do you mean, Marshall?" the president asked.

Marshall pointed to the flower vase on the table. "Someone could have planted a bug!" he whispered.

KC gasped. "Do you think?" She got up and walked around the room, peering into small spaces.

"It's not likely that anyone could have gotten a listening device in here," the president said. "These rooms are very secure."

"Marshall may have a point. I'll have the place swept just to be sure," Mary

Kincaid said. "Meanwhile, will you two be choosing a different place for your honeymoon?"

"Definitely," the president said. He looked across the table at Lois. "How about—"

"Shhh," Lois whispered, grinning. "The walls may have ears. We'll talk about it later."

"At least Darla Darling didn't find out about your dress," KC said to her mother.

Lois smiled. "It's the most beautiful dress in the world," she said. "Michael is a genius!"

During the night, the FBI checked the president's private residence for bugs. They found nothing.

The next morning, a drawing of Lois's wedding dress took up almost all of Darla

Darling's column in the newspaper. There was even a picture of Michael, the man who had designed the dress. The headline over the picture read:

NEW FIRST LADY'S DRESS IS
GRAND, GREEN, AND GORGEOUS!

3

The Stranger's Voice

KC dashed into her mother's bedroom with the newspaper. Lois was still asleep, but not for long.

"Mom, wake up! Look at this!"

Lois rolled over and blinked at her excited daughter. Then she looked at the clock. "Honey, it's only seven o'clock. What's so important?"

"I went downstairs to get the paper. Look!" KC held the newspaper in front of her mother. "They found out about your dress!"

Lois looked at the pictures and read the headline. "Oh my goodness," she whispered. Then she reached for the telephone and called the president.

While her mom showered and dressed, KC called Marshall. He lived in her apartment building, two floors down. The phone rang five times before KC heard someone pick up.

"Niagara Falls, drop over," Marshall's sleepy voice said into KC's ear.

"Have you seen today's newspaper?" KC nearly shouted.

"I'm still in bed, KC," Marshall said. "All I see is my pillow."

"You're not going to believe it," KC said. "Get dressed and meet us in the lobby in fifteen minutes!"

A half hour later, KC, her mom, and Marshall met the president in his private White House rooms. He was sitting at the table in the little kitchen. His hair was messed up and he hadn't shaved. The newspaper was spread out on the table. Yvonne, the president's private maid, set bagels, glasses, and a pitcher of orange juice on the counter, then left the room.

"This is so creepy!" Marshall said, staring at the newspaper. "How did they find out?"

"This drawing of my dress isn't exactly right," Lois muttered. "But it's close enough. And the only people who knew what the dress looked like were the four of us, the vice president, and Michael."

"Maybe Michael told Darla," KC suggested.

Lois shook her head. "No. Michael never talks about his clients. He has to keep secrets, or he wouldn't last long in the dress-designing business. Besides, I never told him where we were going on our honeymoon."

"How about the people who work for him?" the president asked.

"Only Michael knew who the dress was really for," Lois said. "I told him to write L. Smith on the order."

Marshall got himself a bagel and dropped a small piece on the floor. George leaped from the refrigerator to the counter, then to the floor. He pounced on the morsel and carried it to a corner.

"I don't understand it," KC said. "How could someone be listening? Didn't the FBI check for bugs last night?"

"Yes, they gave this place a thorough going-over," the president said.

Lois sighed. "Well, I wanted to keep

my wedding dress a secret, but now the world knows."

"I'm sorry about your dress," the president said. "But if someone has managed to learn our wedding secrets, they might also be overhearing other things we talk about." He glanced around the table. "Like national security."

Marshall's eyes widened. "You mean top-secret information?"

"That's exactly what I mean," President Thornton said. He glanced at Lois. "Maybe we should postpone the wedding till we clear this up."

"You can't cancel the wedding!" KC cried.

"Oh, we'll still get married," the president said. "But maybe we should put it off till we find out what's going on."

"Zachary is right," KC's mom said. "We can hardly go on our honeymoon if there's a spy in the White House!"

"I'll get to the bottom of this mystery," the president said. "Right now, I'm going to get the FBI back in here for another bug check!"

"And I'm going to call the hotel in Hawaii and tell them the Smiths have changed their mind," Lois said. "Then I'll think about a different dress."

The president and KC's mom left the room with George tagging along behind them.

"Come on," KC told Marshall. "I have an idea."

"I do, too," Marshall said, following KC past Arnold and into the hallway. "I want to go to Rock Creek Park. The bugs will just be coming out to sun themselves on the rocks."

"I promise we'll go to the park, just not right now," KC said. "Don't you want to figure out who's spying on my mom and the president?"

"Okay, what's your idea?" Marshall asked as he and KC left the White House.

"We're going to see Darla Darling," KC said.

"That society lady?" Marshall yelped. "Oh, great. Just what I need. She'll probably make us drink tea out of itty-bitty cups. I'll be bored to death!"

"Marsh, Darla Darling started this whole thing," KC said. "She may be the link to whoever is spying on the White House!"

KC and Marshall kept walking along

Pennsylvania Avenue until they reached the offices of the *Star* newspaper. Opposite the front door was a big desk. A woman with blond hair sat there typing at a keyboard. Through a doorway on the right, KC could see people working at computers and talking on telephones. A doorway on the left opened on a long, empty hallway.

The woman with blond hair looked up. "May I help you?" she asked.

"We're here to see Darla Darling," KC said.

The woman squinted at KC. "Do you have an appointment?" she asked. "Ms. Darling is very busy."

"I'm KC Corcoran. My mom is marrying the president," KC said.

The woman's eyes widened. She

reached for her telephone and dialed. "Hello, Darla, there's a Miss Corcoran here to see you. No, not Lois Corcoran. It's her daughter."

Five seconds later, KC and Marshall heard footsteps tapping down the hallway. A tall woman with broad shoulders was striding toward them. She wore a black pants suit and black high-heeled boots. Her dark, curly hair bounced when she walked.

"Hello, I'm Darla Darling," the woman said in a smooth, low voice. Her blue eyes gleamed like wet marbles.

KC had to tilt her head back to see the woman's face. "I'm KC, and this is my friend Marshall," KC said. "We want to talk to you about my mom's wedding."

"Wonderful!" Darla said. "Follow me."

She spun around and strode back down the hallway. KC and Marshall had to practically run to keep up.

At the end of the hall, Darla Darling entered an open doorway. She sat in a swivel chair behind a messy desk. "Have a seat," she said, waving a hand at a pair of purple chairs.

The kids sat. KC glanced around the cluttered office. She saw a computer, a fax machine, two telephones, a tape recorder, a small TV set, and a bunch of other stuff. Papers were scattered across the desk.

Along one wall was a small bed. It was neatly made up with pillows and a bright red cover. Next to the bed were a sink and mirror. Lined up on the sink counter were a toothbrush and toothpaste, a bottle of green mouthwash, and lots of small jars.

Cool, thought KC. *She's so busy she even sleeps here. Someday when I'm a reporter, I'll do that, too!*

Darla Darling flipped open a pad and picked up a pencil. "So, what did you want to tell me?" she asked KC and Marshall.

KC gulped. "I really wanted to ask you something," she said.

Darla Darling leaned forward. "I'm listening."

"How did you find out about my mom's dress and where she was going on her honeymoon?" KC asked.

Ms. Darling's eyes opened wide. "Surely you don't expect me to tell you that?" she asked, smiling. Her teeth were big and white.

"That stuff was a secret," Marshall said. "No one is supposed to know."

Darla shrugged her wide shoulders. "My job is to report the news to my readers," she said. "And when the president gets married, *that's* news!"

"But their honeymoon and Mom's dress were private!" KC said. "The president wants to know how you found out!"

Darla Darling sighed. "All right. Someone telephoned me with the information. I don't know who it was, and even if I did, I wouldn't tell you."

She tapped one of the phones with her pencil. "If I revealed my sources, this phone would stop ringing. I'd be out of business just like that," she said, snapping her fingers.

Darla stood up and walked toward the door. "Now if you'll excuse me, I have a thousand things to do."

KC and Marshall followed her to the door.

"Isn't there anything you can tell us about who called you?" asked KC. "The president really wants to know."

Darla Darling looked down at the two kids. She closed her eyes as if she were trying to remember. Then she smiled.

"Well, I do remember one thing," she said. "The caller had a scratchy voice."

4
Two Suspects

KC and Marshall left the *Star* offices and headed back to the White House.

"That was a waste of time," Marshall said. "We didn't learn anything."

"Yes, we did," KC said. "We know how Darla Darling gets her information."

"But we don't know who's calling her," said Marshall.

"Right, but we do know it's someone with a scratchy voice," said KC.

"How does that help?" Marshall asked. "On TV, spies always try to disguise their voice. This guy probably sounded that way on purpose."

"Okay, you're right," KC said. "But we do know something else. The caller has to be someone close to the president."

"Hey, wait a minute!" Marshall cried. "How about Arnold? He's always standing outside the president's door! And he's got a cold, so his voice is hoarse!"

"Arnold?" KC stopped walking. "Yeah, he could have overheard Mom and the president talking! But why would he tell Darla Darling?"

"For money!" Marshall said. "Maybe she pays him for information."

"But she told us she doesn't know who the caller is," KC said. "How could she pay him?"

Marshall thought for a minute. "Maybe Arnold tells her where to leave the money, then he goes and gets it later. Darla

wouldn't have to know who she was leav-
ing the money for."

The kids kept walking. Soon they were
at the White House. They walked to the
rear parking lot. The private entrance was
near some hedges.

"Look, there's the vice president," KC
said to Marshall. "What's she doing?"

They watched Vice President Kincaid.
She had her hand cupped over her mouth
and was speaking into a cell phone. She
kept glancing around, as if she didn't want
to be overheard. KC tried to eavesdrop,
but she was too far away.

The vice president snapped her phone
shut, crossed the lot, and disappeared into
the White House.

KC stared at the spot where the vice
president had been standing. "You know,

Arnold isn't the only one who's always near the president's door," she said after a minute. "The vice president walks in and out all the time."

"Ms. Kincaid? Why would she spy on the president?" Marshall asked. "I don't think she needs the money."

"I don't know, but Mom showed her the dress a few days ago," KC said. "And the president must have told her where they were going on their honeymoon. Let's keep an eye on her."

The kids entered the White House through the private door. Arnold was stationed outside the president's private rooms.

He sneezed and blew his nose. "Hi, kids," he said.

"How's your cold?" KC asked.

Arnold grinned and stuffed his handkerchief into a pocket. "I think it's getting better," he said.

KC listened to his raspy voice. "Do you know anyone named Darla?" she asked.

"I don't think so. I know a Dora and a Denise, and my sister's name is Debi," he said. "But no Darlas."

He took out a box of lozenges and put one on his tongue. "Want one?" he asked. "They're cough drops, but they taste pretty good. They're called Minti-Meds. I take 'em for my sore throat." Arnold held out the box as he opened the door.

"No thanks," KC said.

When KC and Marshall walked into the president's rooms, they got a shock. KC's mom was crying. The president stood next to her, holding a newspaper.

"Mom, what's wrong?" KC asked. She hurried over to her.

The president held out the paper so KC and Marshall could see Darla Darling's column. The headline was at least five inches tall. It said:

PRESIDENT MAY
CANCEL WEDDING!

"Someone *is* spying on us!" Lois said, wiping her eyes. "They're hearing our private conversations."

"This has gotten serious," the president said. "No one but us was part of that conversation." He dropped into a chair. "I can't believe someone on my staff is a spy, but if I have to, I'll fire everyone."

"Um, Marsh and I have an idea who it

might be," KC said. She told her mother and the president what Darla Darling had said about her secret caller.

"Someone is giving Darla information over the phone?" Lois said.

"Someone with a scratchy voice!" Marshall went on.

"Yeah, and guess who has a cold?" KC whispered. She pointed to the door through which they'd walked. "Arnold!"

Four pairs of eyes looked at the door.

"Arnold?" the president said. "Well, he is always just outside that door, so he could have overheard, I suppose."

"Someone else knows all your secrets," KC said.

"I'm not sure I want to hear this," the president said. "Okay, who?"

"The vice president," KC whispered.

5
The Truth

"Mary?" the president said. "But she wouldn't . . . I mean, I trust her!"

"Zachary, she *has* seen my dress, and I know we told her where we were going for our honeymoon," KC's mom said.

The president shook his head. "No. I've known Mary for years," he said.

"Could she have told someone without meaning to?" Marshall asked. "Maybe she was just talking, and she accidentally blabbed everything. It happens!"

"I find that hard to believe," Lois said. "I think someone is spying on us. We have to find out who!"

"I have an idea," KC said.

The president rubbed his temples, as if he had a headache. "Tell me. I'll try anything to get to the bottom of this."

KC explained her idea.

"I like it," the president said a minute later. He stood up, crossed the room, and opened his door. "Arnold, may I speak to you in here, please?"

"Yes, sir!" Arnold said with a hoarse voice. He stepped smartly into the room and stood at attention. George the cat followed Arnold inside and flopped on the rug under the president's chair.

"Relax, Arnold," the president said. "I just wanted to tell you something so you're not taken by surprise. Because of all this unwanted publicity, Ms. Corcoran and I have decided to elope. After we're married, we'll just disappear for a short honeymoon."

Arnold's eyes widened, but he didn't say a word.

"Please keep this to yourself, Arnold," the president said. "It's absolutely top-secret! You may go now, and I hope you're taking something for your cold."

"Yes, sir, I am," Arnold said. Then he snapped off a salute, about-faced, and marched out of the room.

"How did I do?" the president asked.

"You did great," Lois said.

"One down, one to go," the president said. He picked up his telephone and pressed a button. "Mary, would you come in for a minute, please?"

The vice president walked into the office through another door. She smiled at

Lois and the kids. "Yes, Mr. President?"

"I have some news about our wedding," the president said.

KC was sitting behind the president. She saw him cross his fingers behind his back.

"I hope this Darla Darling business hasn't made you change your plans," Mary Kincaid said.

"Actually, we *have* made new plans," the president said. "Lois and I are going to elope. We'll be gone for a few days."

Mary Kincaid raised her eyebrows at the news.

"We are the only five who know," the president said. He grinned at his vice president. "And we don't want Darla Darling to be the sixth."

"Of course, sir," Mary Kincaid said. She

closed an imaginary zipper over her lips.

"Fine," the president said. "I'll let you know more as we work out the details."

"Thank you for confiding in me," Mary said. She nodded and left the room. George walked out with the vice president, rubbing against her ankles.

"I feel like a lying skunk," the president said when the door closed.

"Nobody likes to lie," Lois said. "But if this information makes it into Ms. Darling's column, at least we'll know either Arnold or Mary is our spy."

"Yeah," the president grumbled. "My personal guard or my vice president. Great!"

The next morning, still in her slippers, KC took the elevator down to the lobby of her building. She hoped the newspapers had arrived.

They had! A small stack sat on a table outside the elevator doors. KC snatched the top one and jumped back in before the doors closed. She found Darla Darling's column and grinned.

Instead of going back up to her apartment, KC got off on Marshall's floor. She rang his bell as she looked at what Darla had written.

Marshall came to the door barefoot, wearing Spider-Man pajamas.

"Good morning, Spider-Man," KC said. "Read this and get dressed!"

"Can I finish my breakfast first?" Marshall asked.

"Sure, but hurry up, okay?"

Marshall padded to his kitchen with

KC behind him, rattling the newspaper.

Marshall sat and spooned up his cereal. "Is it in there?" he asked, pointing his spoon at the paper.

KC nodded and slid the paper in front of Marshall. There was Darla's smiling face. Beneath her picture a bold headline read:

PRESIDENT AND FIANCÉE
PLAN TO ELOPE!
WATCH MY COLUMN FOR MORE!

"Oh my gosh!" Marshall said. "We were right. It *is* Arnold or Vice President Kincaid! The president is going to flip!"

"That's why you have to hurry up," KC said. "We have to find the snitch before he or she ruins my wedding!"

6
Spying on Spies

Marshall grinned as he slurped up the last spoonful. "*Your* wedding?"

"You know what I mean," KC said. She began pacing back and forth. "We still don't know which one is the spy. We have to catch him or her with the goods."

Marshall put his bowl and spoon in the sink. "What goods?"

"The money, Marshall. Maybe we can catch Arnold or the vice president taking money from Darla."

"KC, we can't follow Arnold. He drives a fast motorcycle, and we don't even know where he lives."

"Okay, but we can spy on the vice president," KC said.

Marshall grinned. "Spying on a spy? I like that."

"Will you get dressed and help?" KC asked. "I don't want Mom to cancel her wedding."

Marshall closed one eye and stared at KC out of the other. "Okay. But promise me we'll go to the park after they're married." He stuck out his pinkie.

KC put out her pinkie. "Promise!" she said. They shook pinkies, and Marshall went to change.

They rushed to the White House and hurried toward the president's private rooms. A marine stood guard at the door, but it wasn't Arnold.

The guard clicked his heels together

when he saw KC and Marshall. "Good morning," he said. "Can I help you?"

"Hi," KC said, surprised to see this short marine instead of tall Arnold. "Have you seen the vice president?"

"No, miss. I just relieved Arnold, and I haven't seen anyone yet but you two." The guard held the door open for them.

In the kitchen, Yvonne was cleaning up. "Good morning. I have a note for you," she told KC. She pulled a folded piece of paper from her uniform pocket.

KC read it out loud to Marshall. *Honey—Zachary and I need some time alone to talk about the wedding. We may be back late. Love, Mom.*

"I left your lunch in the fridge," Yvonne said. "And there's a bowl of fruit on the table."

"Thanks, Yvonne," KC said. "Did they say where they were going?"

"No, miss," Yvonne said. "But I know they took a private car." She hesitated. "They looked pretty unhappy, miss!"

"Um, have you seen the vice president yet this morning?" KC asked.

"No, miss," Yvonne said. She left KC and Marshall in the sunny kitchen. George slipped into the room behind the maid's heels.

As soon as Yvonne was gone, KC grabbed Marshall by the arm. "Now's our chance!" she hissed.

"For what?" he sighed.

"Now's our chance to snoop!" KC said.

"You've been snooping your whole life!" Marshall said. "What's so different today?" He reached for a banana.

"We don't have time to eat," KC said. "If the vice president isn't here yet, we can check out her office!"

"For what?" Marshall said again, dropping the banana.

"I don't know, but if she's selling information to Darla Darling, we might see some evidence," KC said.

The kids walked down the hall toward the vice president's office. A large statue of a Native American family stood next to her door, which was partly open.

KC stuck her nose around the corner and nearly fainted. The vice president was standing with her back to the door, talking on a cell phone.

KC grabbed Marshall, and they both hid behind the statue.

Just then the vice president came

through the door. She walked toward the Oval Office, still talking into her phone.

"I know that," Mary Kincaid was saying. "But this has to be kept secret. . . ."

When she was a few yards away, KC whispered, "Let's try to find out who she's talking to!"

Tiptoeing, they followed the vice president. She passed the Oval Office, still quietly speaking into her phone.

Then she stopped and started to turn around.

Panicking, KC looked for someplace to hide. The closest doorway led to the Oval Office. She knew it would be empty, because the president had left with her mom.

KC poked Marshall, and they both scooted into the Oval Office. There was a

big desk, a few chairs, and a long sofa. A tall plant stood in front of the window.

"This is spooking me out," Marshall whispered. "There has to be a federal law about breaking into the president's office."

"We didn't break in, Marsh," KC said. "Besides, next week, I'll be living in this place."

"Yeah, if we're both not living in jail!" Marshall said.

Suddenly Marshall grabbed KC's hand and yanked her down behind the president's desk.

KC started to protest, but Marshall's hand was across her mouth. She looked at him, trying to figure out what was going on. Marshall's eyes were as big as pancakes.

Then KC understood. She heard footsteps whisper across the carpet. She saw a shadow fall on the wall behind her.

Someone else was checking out the Oval Office!

7

Motorcycle Meeting

KC and Marshall froze behind the desk. They hardly breathed as they heard papers being moved above their heads. Then the shadow moved away.

KC heard the office door open, then close. She crawled from behind the desk and raced for the door.

"What're you doing?" Marshall asked.

"I want to see who that was!" KC hissed. "And what they stole off the president's desk!"

KC slowly eased the door open. She stuck her head out, then back in, like a redheaded turtle.

"It's the vice president!" KC said.

Marshall blinked. "So? She can go into the Oval Office if she wants," he said.

"Come on!" KC said. "Let's follow her."

Walking as quietly as possible, the kids sneaked after the vice president. She left the building and walked toward the employee parking lot. KC and Marshall followed. When she sat on a bench and took out her cell phone, they hid behind some bushes.

"What's she doing?" Marshall asked.

"Talking on her phone again," KC said.

Suddenly they heard a roar. A motorcycle pulled up in front of the bench. When the driver removed his helmet, the kids saw that it was Arnold.

The vice president stood up and slipped her cell phone into her pocket.

From her bag, she took out a small package and handed it to Arnold. They spoke for a minute. Then he put on his helmet and zoomed out of the parking lot. After a few seconds, the vice president hurried back into the building.

"They must both be in on it!" KC said, stepping out from behind the bushes. "Whatever she took off the president's desk, she just gave it to Arnold!"

"And he'll give it to Darla Darling," Marshall said.

KC nodded. "We know it now, but how do we prove it?" she asked.

"I can't prove anything on an empty stomach," Marshall said.

"Okay, come on," KC said. "How can you eat? Don't you feel bad? I really like Arnold and the vice president."

"I like them, too," Marshall said. Then his stomach rumbled.

In the president's kitchen, KC and Marshall sat down at the table. Marshall peeled a banana and started to eat.

George was lying on the counter next to the refrigerator. His bushy tail swept back and forth.

Both kids watched George as he reached for a mouse refrigerator magnet.

The magnet fell to the floor. In a flash, George pounced. He grabbed the mouse in his paws and began chewing on the plastic.

"No, George!" KC said. "Spit it out!" She got down on her knees and moved toward the cat. George jumped up and walked away.

"Now what did you do with that silly

magnet?" KC asked, looking at the floor.

"Maybe it's in his mouth," Marshall said. He slipped behind George and grabbed him.

KC sat on the floor beside Marshall and tried to make George open his mouth.

"Here it is," Marshall said. "It's stuck on his collar."

He pulled the magnet loose and held it out to KC. But she was examining George's collar.

"How could a magnet stick to a plastic collar?" she asked. Slowly, she slid the collar around, studying it closely.

Suddenly KC gasped. She yanked her hands away from the collar as if it were red-hot.

"What?" Marshall asked.

With shaking hands, KC unbuckled George's collar. She opened a drawer, laid the collar inside, and quietly slid the drawer shut. Then she scooted down next to Marshall again.

"KC, are you gonna tell me what's going on?" Marshall asked. "You look all funny."

"That plastic collar has a round metal thing on it," KC whispered. "That's what the magnet was sticking to."

"So? Why do you look so weird?" Marshall asked.

"That piece of metal is a bug," KC said. "A listening device!"

Marshall blinked about seven times. "So . . . someone bugged George? A *cat* is the spy in the White House?"

KC nodded. "George is usually with

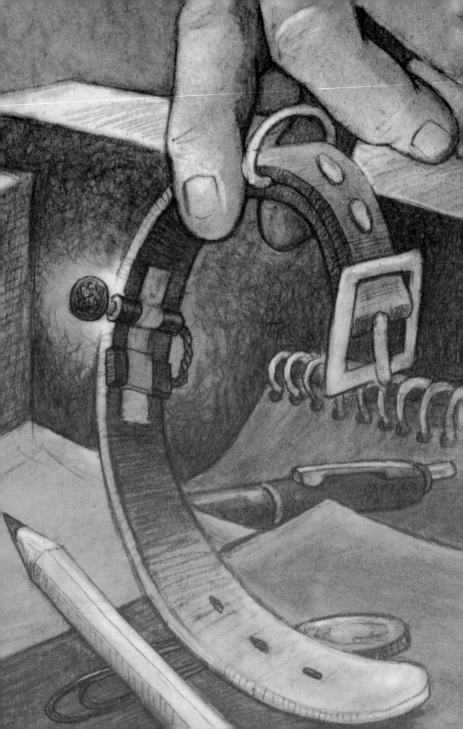

the president. That must be how the spy found out all the wedding stuff and reported it to Darla Darling!" she said.

"But who did it?" Marshall asked.

KC shrugged. "It could be anyone who can get close to George," she said. The cat looked at Marshall and meowed.

"So the snitch isn't Arnold or the vice president?" asked Marshall.

"It could still be one of them," KC said. "But I doubt it. They're both here all the time, so why would they have to bug George? But it could be anyone else who works here."

Marshall groaned. "What do we do now? I sure wish the president were here!" he said.

"Well, he's not, but you just gave me a great idea!" KC said. "We can pretend the president is here. And I think I know a way to make the spy come here, too!"

"Am I gonna like this?" Marshall asked, looking worried.

KC beamed. "You're gonna hate it!"

She opened the drawer, lifted out the collar, and carefully placed her hand over the little metal bug. Then she slid next to Marshall. "Just go along with whatever I say," she whispered in his ear.

Marshall gulped, staring at the collar. "You mean we're gonna talk to that thing?"

KC nodded. "Pretend you're in a school play," she said.

"Oh, great," Marshall said. "The last time I was in a play, I got so nervous I nearly puked."

"Well, no puking this time," KC said.

"We have to sound normal. Are you ready?"

Marshall swallowed. "I guess so," he muttered.

KC took her hand off the bug. "Isn't it exciting that Mom and the president are eloping today?" she said with her mouth near the collar.

KC nudged Marshall's foot and placed the collar in his lap.

Marshall's mouth fell open. He stared at the collar as if it were a rattlesnake. He tried to swallow, but his mouth was dry.

KC kicked his foot again. She mouthed the words, *Say something! Someone is listening!*

Marshall took a deep breath before he spoke into the collar. "Yeah, but it's too b-bad they're n-not having their big w-wedding. I was really looking forward to all that c-cake and ice cream."

KC smiled at Marshall and took the collar back. "They have to do it this way to make sure Darla Darling doesn't find out the new honeymoon spot," she said, speaking into the little listening device.

"What time are they eloping?" asked Marshall, taking the collar back. He had stopped stuttering. KC could tell he was getting into it now.

KC glanced up at the kitchen clock. It was almost noon. "Two o'clock," she said, leaning over the collar.

"How are they getting there?" Marshall asked, trying to stop himself from cracking up. "In the president's private plane?"

KC snatched the cat's collar out of Marshall's hands.

"The president doesn't want anyone to recognize him," she said. "He'll be in a taxi and wearing a baseball cap and dark glasses. Mom will have a red scarf over her hair. He's picking her up at the side entrance, near those tall bushes."

Marsh started to giggle, so KC put the collar back in the drawer.

"That was so cool!" Marshall said. "I feel like we're in a James Bond movie!"

"I don't think James Bond giggles," KC said.

"Now what do we do?" Marshall asked.

"We wait till two o'clock," KC said. "And keep our fingers crossed that the spy overheard us and comes to see the president and Mom eloping!"

KC told Marshall the rest of her plan.

Marshall grinned. "I like it," he said.

"Except for one thing. What happens when the spy gets here at two and there's no president and no taxi and no eloping?"

KC looked at him blankly. "Oh," she said. "I didn't think of that."

Marshall sighed. "Good thing James Bond is here to help you." He stood up and reached for the phone. "Here," he said. "Call a taxi."

8
The Fish Takes the Bait!

At ten minutes before two o'clock, KC and Marshall slipped out of the White House. They hid in the bushes near the president's private driveway. KC had her camera.

"What if the spy doesn't show up?" Marshall asked.

"If the spy heard us talking, he or she won't be able to resist!" KC said. "When the president elopes, that's big news! And I'm sure Darla would pay for it."

She looked at her watch. "The taxi should be here any minute. I hope Yvonne is watching."

As if by magic, a taxi slowed and pulled to a stop only a few yards from where KC and Marshall were hiding.

The driver got out and opened the taxi trunk. He was wearing a baseball cap and dark glasses. Following KC's instructions, the driver whistled.

"Get ready," KC mumbled to Marshall.

A woman in a trench coat and red scarf walked briskly out of the side entrance of the White House. She was carrying a small suitcase and wore sunglasses.

"Yvonne looks just like your mother!" Marshall marveled.

"Yeah," KC said, grinning.

Just as Yvonne reached the taxi, KC and Marshall heard a roar. A black motor-cycle zoomed up and screeched to a stop five feet behind the taxi. The person on the bike wore a black leather jacket and pants and a matching helmet. A visor hid the rider's face.

"It's Arnold!" Marshall whispered.

The motorcycle rider straddled the bike. With hands hidden by black leather gloves, he flipped up the visor.

KC saw lipstick and dark curly hair. "No, it's the vice president!" she said.

With the motor still running, the cyclist pulled a small camera from a pocket and snapped a picture of the taxi driver and Yvonne.

KC jumped out of the bushes, her own camera aimed at the motorcycle. "Smile!" she yelled.

The startled rider whipped around and looked at KC. They were only a few feet apart.

KC let out a gasp.

The motorcycle rider wasn't Arnold.

It wasn't the vice president, either.

"Hi, Ms. Darling," KC said.

Darla Darling glared at KC, then flipped down her visor and gunned her engine. With squealing tires, the bike and its rider disappeared into the traffic.

An hour later, the president and KC's mom came back. Yvonne brought them all lemonade in the president's private kitchen. George—without his collar—sat on the president's lap. He purred as his ears were stroked.

"I hope you don't mind me wearing your scarf and sunglasses," Yvonne said to Lois.

"Mind? I think it was a wonderful

idea!" Lois said. "Thank you for your help."

"You're very welcome," Yvonne said, blushing, as she left the room.

"So you told the taxi driver to dress like me, and Yvonne pretended to be your mother," the president said. "And when Darla heard we were eloping today, she shot over here to get the scoop."

KC nodded. "I guess Darla put the bug on George's collar when he got away from us in the rose garden. She must have known that was the only way to bug the White House."

"So it was Darla all the time," KC's mom said. "There was no caller with a scratchy voice. She sat in her office and listened to us talking, then wrote her columns."

"And my own *cat* was the spy!" the president said.

Marshall laughed. "We knew the spy had to be someone near you," he said. "And George is always sitting on your lap."

KC looked at Marshall. "Do you remember when I smelled something minty on George's fur?" she asked. "It was from Darla's mouthwash."

"Mary Kincaid will get quite a chuckle when I tell her you kids thought she might be the motorcycle-riding spy," the president said.

"Do you have to tell her?" KC asked, embarrassed.

"Don't worry," said the president. "She'll be thrilled to know that you kids came to the rescue."

"I wonder what she was giving Arnold in the parking lot?" Marshall asked.

"One way to find out," the president said. He shooed George off his lap and walked over to the door. When he opened the door, Arnold was sipping soup from a mug.

"Arnold, will you step in here, please?"

Arnold came into the room. "Sir?" he said.

The president quickly told Arnold how KC and Marshall had solved the mystery of the White House spy. "But they're wondering what the vice president handed you in the parking lot."

Arnold grinned and held up the soup. "This," he said. "And cough syrup. Ms. Kincaid brings me something every day!"

"What will happen to Darla Darling?"

Marshall asked after Arnold left the room.

"I'm sure the FBI will have a talk with her about the incident," the president said sternly. For a moment, KC felt sorry for Darla. "But no harm done in the long run," the president went on. "We may even invite her to the wedding."

"You *are* getting married!" KC yelled.

"Yes," her mother said. "Saturday at three o'clock. I've decided to wear the green dress, after all. And that night, we'll be in Paris, France!"

9

The Cat Wore White

KC peeked out from behind a tent pole to check out the rose garden. Wooden folding chairs had been set up on the lawn. A long red carpet ran up the aisle.

KC's and her mom's green dresses were the same color as Marshall's vest and the president's bow tie.

A platform had been placed at the back of the garden for the band. They played happy tunes while the guests waited for Lois to walk down the aisle.

At the other end of the red carpet, the president stood by Reverend Murphy, waiting.

"Doesn't the president look nice?" KC whispered to Marshall.

"He looks great, but I feel dorky in this vest," Marshall said.

"I think it's cute," KC said.

"Yeah, right," Marshall said. He held one end of a long green ribbon. The other end was tied to the ring box attached to George's new white collar.

George lay on the carpet, chewing on his ribbon. His tail flipped back and forth. "Please don't run away again," KC begged him.

The wedding ceremony started. Then it was time for KC and Marshall to walk George forward with the rings.

As they marched slowly along the carpet, KC smiled at the vice president, Arnold, and Yvonne.

Darla Darling sat with the other re-porters in the press seats. She was busy taking notes. She wasn't even watching the wedding. KC almost giggled, wondering where she parked her motorcycle.

KC stopped at the end of the aisle. Marshall stood next to the president. George rolled over onto his back and stared out at the crowd.

The band started playing the wedding march. KC's mom walked down the aisle in her beautiful dress. Everyone stood and clapped.

When Reverend Murphy nodded, Lois passed her bouquet to KC. Then Marshall opened George's little box and handed the wedding rings to the president.

The couple said, "I do!"

"I now pronounce you husband and

wife!" said Reverend Murphy. The president kissed KC's mom, and everyone cheered.

A few minutes later, the chairs were moved away, and a wooden dance floor was laid over the grass. Waiters brought out food, and the band began playing dance music.

KC watched the president lead her mother onto the dance floor. Once they had begun dancing, all the guests joined in. KC smiled when she saw Arnold dancing with Yvonne.

KC walked up to Marshall. "Do you want to dance?" she asked.

Marshall set his punch cup on a table.

He looked into KC's big green eyes.

Then he ran out of the rose garden as fast as his legs would carry him.

This is the end of
A SPY IN THE
WHITE HOUSE.

Turn the page to read the first chapter of

THE SECRET AT
JEFFERSON'S MANSION.

1
The Hidden Cupboard

"Marsh, I can't see anything in here!" KC said. "Hand me the flashlight."

Marshall Li grinned. "It doesn't work," he fibbed. "The batteries must be dead. Better watch out for spiders. They love to hide in dark places."

KC backed out of her bedroom closet. "I just changed those batteries last week," she told him. She took the flashlight from Marshall and switched it on.

"Don't try to scare me," she said. "Spiders are gross, but I'm not afraid of them."

"Spiders aren't gross!" Marshall said. "They're smart and shy and wouldn't hurt a fly . . . well, maybe they would."

Marshall loved all creatures, but especially those with eight legs. He had a pet tarantula and hoped to work in the insect zoo at the Smithsonian someday.

KC Corcoran was President Zachary Thornton's stepdaughter. KC had moved into the White House when her mother and the president got married. Marshall Li, who lived nearby, was KC's best friend.

KC had decided to paint the inside of her closet, and Marshall was helping her. They piled all her clothes on KC's bed.

KC had brought cleaning rags and a stepladder from the kitchen.

"Come on, let's get started," she said to Marshall. They each grabbed a dustcloth and crowded into the closet. KC set the flashlight on top of the stepladder.

"Why isn't there a light in your closet?"

Marshall asked. "Mine at home has one."

"This is one of the oldest bedrooms in the White House," KC said. She wiped dust and cobwebs from the wall in front of her. "There was no electricity when it was built. I guess they just forgot about the closet when electricity was added to the White House."

Marshall climbed up the stepladder and aimed the flashlight around the space. He paused when it shone on one corner.

"Hey, what's that thing on the wall?" Marshall pointed to a small lump under the paint. It was perfectly round and the size of a half-dollar.

Marshall tapped the bump with the end of the flashlight. Some of the old paint flaked off. He looked at the bump more closely. "I think it's a ring," he said. He wiggled a finger under the paint and tugged. Suddenly a square piece of wall came away in his hand. He jumped off the stepladder as paint flakes fell onto his hair.

"Let me see!" KC took his place on the ladder. She shone her flashlight into a square hole in the closet wall. "It's a secret cubbyhole!" she said.

"Is there anything inside?" Marshall asked, wiping dust and paint off his shirt.

"Cobwebs," KC said. "And a couple of shelves." She stood on the top step and reached into the hole. The shelves were deep, so she had to shove her whole arm in.

KC felt a sharp edge. "I think there's something in here! It feels like some kind of box," she said.

"Maybe it's a pirate's chest filled with treasure," Marshall cracked.

"Here, take the light." KC handed the flashlight to Marshall so she'd have both hands free. She slid the thing forward and pulled it into the closet. It was a chest, but not a pirate's. About the size of a pizza box, it was made of wood and stood only six inches high.

KC set the box on top of the stepladder next to her. She wiped dust and grime off the wood.

"I wonder what's in it," Marshall whispered. He tried to lift the lid. "It won't open."

KC noticed a small round hole. "Maybe this is a lock," she said.

She thrust the chest into Marshall's arms and reached all the way into the corners of the hole. She ran her fingers across the rough wood.

"Found something," KC muttered. She brought her hand out, holding a small key.

KC's heart was beating wildly. She put the key into the small hole of the box and turned it. When he heard a click, Marshall lifted the lid.

Inside were twelve small horses. Each was about six inches long. They were different colors. Some were wooden. Some were made of clay. One was made of cardboard and twigs tied together with string. Each horse lay in its own pocket, like chocolates in a box. They looked old.

"Cool!" Marshall said.

KC wiped the inside of the box lid. "Someone wrote something here," she said.

Marshall ran his fingers over the words. "The letters are carved," he said.

THESE HORSES WERE CREATED

AND GIVEN TO ME BY MY DEAR
GRANDCHILDREN.

OF ALL MY WORLDLY GOODS,
THESE I TREASURE THE MOST.

Beneath the message were a signature
and a date:

THOMAS JEFFERSON, 1808

"Oh my gosh!" KC said. "These horses
belonged to Thomas Jefferson!"

"How'd they get stuck in this closet?"
Marshall wondered out loud.

"Maybe his grandchildren put them
there," KC suggested.

She gently picked up one of the clay
horses. "Just think, some little kid made
this about two hundred years ago," she
said. "Come on, we have to show these to
my mom and the president!"

KC placed the horse back in its spot,

and the kids raced down the hallway. They found the president and KC's mom in the private library, playing Scrabble. The three White House cats were each curled in a ball on the sofa.

"I don't think 'pid' is a word, dear," Lois said to KC's stepfather, the president.

"Yes, it is," President Thornton said confidently.

"Then use it in a sentence," the First Lady said. She winked at KC and Marshall.

"'Pid' is short for 'pigeon,'" the president said. "The pid flew into its nest."

"Oh, pooh," KC's mom said. "You lose a turn for trying to cheat!"

The president grinned. "Busted," he said. "What have you got there, KC?"

"Can you move the Scrabble board?" KC said.

The president slid the board to one side, and KC set the box on the table.

"We found it in KC's closet!" Marshall said. "It was hidden inside a wall."

KC opened the box, revealing the twelve little horses.

"Oh, how charming!" Lois said.

"Look what's written here!" KC said. She showed them the words Jefferson had carved into the wood.

The president read the words softly. "Amazing," he said.

Lois lifted one of the horses from its pocket. "How do you suppose these got in that closet?" she asked.

"Thomas Jefferson left the White House in 1809," President Thornton said. "I'm sure that ending his presidency and moving out was a confusing time. Imagine the servants loading all Jefferson's boxes and furniture into horse-drawn carriages. Maybe that closet just got overlooked."

KC stroked a little gray horse. "What should we do with them?" she asked.

Lois replaced the horse she'd been holding. She looked at the president. "Any ideas?"

"Yes," the president said. "These horses belong to Thomas Jefferson. They should go to his home, Monticello."

"I thought he lived in the White House," Marshall said.

"He did, for the eight years that he was president," President Thornton said. "But Monticello was his home before he became our third president. After he left the White House, he went back there to live."

"Cool," Marshall said.

"Can we take them there?" KC asked.

"I have meetings all next week," said the president. "But you kids can go with Lois."

KC's mom opened a table drawer and pulled out her calendar. She flipped over a few pages. "We can go on Wednesday," she said. "It'll be a great opportunity for you to see Monticello."

"Where is it?" Marshall asked.

"Monticello is in Virginia," the president said. "A little more than a hundred miles from here."

"I'll work it out with your parents, Marshall," Lois said. "We'll stay overnight near Monticello. It'll be a wonderful adventure. But first you have to get that closet painted!"

Read all of KC and Marshall's adventures
in Washington, D.C.!

Capital Mysteries

Calendar Mysteries

Help Bradley, Brian, Lucy,
and Nate . . .

. . . solve a mystery
a month!

A to Z Mysteries®

Help Dink, Josh, and Ruth Rose . . .

ABOUT THE AUTHOR

Ron Roy has been writing books for children since 1974. He is the author of dozens of books, including the bestselling A to Z Mysteries and Capital Mysteries. He lives in Connecticut with his dog, Pal. When not working on a new book, Ron likes to teach his dog tricks, play poker with friends, travel, and read thrilling mystery books. You can visit Ron on his Web site at www.ronroy.com.